The woman was smart. She had quick wit and a sharp take on life. She also happened to be incredibly beautiful.

Her looks were simply a bonus.

He extended his hand. "Welcome aboard. When can you start?"

She shook his hand. "Tomorrow?"

"Great. Do you have time to stop by HR to do the paperwork right now? That way we can get the formalities out of the way."

They paused by his office door and he could smell her perfume—a hint of roses and spice. She smelled so good, he had to resist the urge to lean in.

Brand me inappropriate all day long.

Now that he'd brought her on board, he would be able to put his business hat back on and be her boss. Strictly her boss, which meant no fraternizing.

But that didn't mean he couldn't enjoy looking at her.

Dear Reader,

The James Lane Allen quote "Adversity does not build character—it reveals it" was a big inspiration for this story. I started thinking about what it would be like to start over after losing everything. Even more so, what would it be like to have it all and lose everything?

That's what happens to Pepper Merriweather, the heroine of *Texas Christmas,* the third book in the Celebrations, Inc., series. When the collapse of her father's empire leaves a stain on the family name, Pepper has no choice but to start over and rebuild her life. In doing so, she discovers she's capable of a whole lot more than she originally thought possible.

When society turns its back on Pepper, Rob Macintyre knows she isn't responsible for her father's sins. With his help, Pepper learns that losing everything is the start to excavating what is important.

I hope you enjoy reading *Texas Christmas* as much as I enjoyed writing it. Please drop me a line at nrobardsthompson@yahoo.com to let me know what you think.

Warmly,

Nancy Robards Thompson

TEXAS CHRISTMAS

*NANCY ROBARDS
THOMPSON*

HARLEQUIN®
entertain, enrich, inspire™

Recycling programs
for this product may
not exist in your area.

ISBN-13: 978-0-373-65706-3

TEXAS CHRISTMAS

Copyright © 2012 by Nancy Robards Thompson

This edition published by arrangement with Harlequin Books S.A.

For questions and comments about the quality of this book,
please contact us at CustomerService@Harlequin.com.

® and TM are trademarks of Harlequin Enterprises Limited or its corporate affiliates. Trademarks indicated with ® are registered in the United States Patent and Trademark Office, the Canadian Trade Marks Office and in other countries.

www.Harlequin.com

Printed in U.S.A.

NANCY ROBARDS THOMPSON

Award-winning author Nancy Robards Thompson is a sister, wife and mother who has lived the majority of her life south of the Mason-Dixon line. As the oldest sibling, she reveled in her ability to make her brother laugh at inappropriate moments, and she soon learned she could get away with it by proclaiming, "What? I wasn't doing anything." It's no wonder that upon graduating from college with a degree in journalism, she discovered that reporting "just the facts" bored her silly. Since she hung up her press pass to write novels full-time, critics have deemed her books "funny, smart and observant." She loves chocolate, champagne, cats and art (though not necessarily in that order). When she's not writing, she enjoys spending time with her family, reading, hiking and doing yoga.

This book is dedicated to Elizabeth Grainger,
whose thoughtful critiquing and generous sharing
helped make me a better writer.
You will be missed, but never forgotten.

Prologue

Maya LeBlanc dusted the batch of white chocolate truffles with a sprinkle of crushed pink rose petals and edible gold dust. As the glittering potpourri rained down from her fingertips, she infused it with a love wish.

The rose petals represented passion and romance, of course. The gold dust, which shimmered in the sunlight that streamed in through the window on the stucco wall above Maya's marble-topped worktable, was for prosperity. And, as if the fine golden powder were in cahoots with the intention at the heart of her handiwork, it shimmered and winked up at her conspiratorially.

Europeans had a long-standing love affair with edible gold. Alchemists believed it was good for the heart. Royalty adorned fruits and other delicacies with it to sustain the health of their hearts. The Elizabethans created sumptuous banquets by adding edible gold dust to fruits such as oranges, grapes, pomegranates and dates and figs.

But Maya's creation was intended for loftier purposes than feeding royals; it was meant to conjure true love.

Ardent, passionate love.

The thought warmed Maya from the inside out, and she smiled with quiet satisfaction as she stepped back to admire her handiwork.

Yes, this was a particularly beautiful batch of chocolate. However, just who would receive the dozen bonbons wasn't quite clear…yet.

The answer had not yet revealed itself, but it would come in due time. Of that, Maya was sure. There was no mistaking that the *winds of love* had danced around her this morning as she'd walked down the ancient cobblestone streets of St. Michel on her way to open the shop. When the winds had called her to action, there was no resting until she'd filled the heavenly order. She wouldn't rest until she'd done everything in her power to bring *the intendeds* together.

Whoever these *intendeds* might be.

Excitement, shimmering as brightly as the gold

dust, shook her. Finding the lucky couple who belonged to these chocolates would be the reward for her hard work.

But first things first. Right now, she had to finish her work. Since the truffles weren't quite set, she pondered whether or not she should add another element…or two, perhaps? Maya surveyed the bunches of twine-tied dried herbs and flowers hanging from wrought-iron rods suspended above her workbench. There was lavender that had dried to a wiry grayish-purple, looking like veins that stood out on an old crone's hand. Lavender denoted purity, silence, devotion and…*caution*.

Non. It didn't fit. Maya's intuitive heart insisted that that this batch of *chocolat* was intended for true love that thrived on passion. Lovers whom fate would send careening toward each other; a lovely collision resulting in two hearts becoming one. She sighed in breathless delight, her hand fluttering to her heart.

Caution would never do.

Her gaze lingered on several fat bunches of rosemary that were bound so tightly they bristled out like small hedgehogs. Rosemary signified remembrance. While it was a sweet sentiment, it didn't quite fit this order, either. Besides, the robust fragrance would overpower the delicate rosewater she'd used in the recipe.

Non. She gave her head a resolute shake. Rosemary wouldn't do, either.

She purposely averted her gaze from the bouquet of dried yellow chrysanthemums because that flower meant *love slighted.* It wasn't as if merely looking at the flowers would infuse the chocolates with bad juju, but when crafting an aromatic enticement for something so delicate as *l'amour du cœur,* one could never be too careful.

Maya, of all people, knew that. As a third generation *chocolatier* and *un marieur*—a matchmaker— she listed chocolate and love, not necessarily in that order, as her passions. But chocolate paid the bills and afforded her the pleasure of answering the call when the winds of love blew in, summoning her to work. It was a challenge she couldn't resist, and she wouldn't rest until her job was done.

In the realm of matchmaking, many factors were out of Maya's control. With that in mind, she'd adopted the philosophy that she was simply the messenger. Still, she always approached her work with care and vigilance, because matters of the heart were as delicate and fragile as spun sugar.

Her gaze danced over the dried flowers and herbs one last time. When nothing spoke to her, she went completely still for a moment and listened to the communiqué her heart had been receiving since she'd awoken that morning with the urgency to whip up this special concoction.

Keep it simple. Rose petals and gold dust. Fini.

As she opened her eyes she was compelled to pick up one more pinch of gold. She blew it off her fingertips, infusing it with another wish and a prayer…for true love of the purest, most selfless sort.

Chapter One

As Pepper Merriweather entered the shop, a sudden, strong gust of December wind blew in, rocking the sign that was adorned with garland and red Christmas ornaments and hung above the shop's door. It read Maya's Chocolates ~ Happily Ever After Starts Here. The wind ballooned the lace curtains on the window and made the bells on the door dance with extra life. Pepper tightened her grip on the brass handle so the glass door wouldn't slam back against the building's ancient stone facade.

The momentary struggle felt like she was arm-wrestling with Mother Nature. When the biting wind finally let up, it felt good to prevail, as if fate were finally cutting her a break.

Silly thought, she mused, as she stepped inside and eased the door shut. The last thing she wanted to do these days was draw attention to herself. Sheepishly, she glanced around the shop. To her relief, the cluttered sales floor proved to be as empty as the cobblestone street behind her.

Despite the principality being dressed in all its Christmas finery and like something from a medieval holiday fairy tale, December was the off-season in St. Michel. Mostly the locals were the lucky ones to enjoy the twinkle lights strung from building to building, the giant, decorated Christmas tree that stood as the centerpiece in the center of town, and the shop windows all decorated for Christmas. The decorations always went up on December first, rain or shine.

During the cold months, foot traffic was lighter in the quaint little village. That's why it had been such a great escape for Pepper, and also why Maya was usually the only one tending the store. That was probably why Pepper didn't see anyone standing behind the counter or out on the floor of the small shop.

"Bonjour?" she called. As if answering, the wind outside gusted another chanson. The shop sign creaked in harmony with the blustery phrases.

"Bonjour!" a muffled voice answered, trailing from the back room. "I'll be right with you."

Pepper stepped away from the door, and a quiet calm settled over the shop. She glanced around at the baker's racks, rough-hewn wooden tables and glass and wrought-iron fixtures that held red-and-green cellophane-wrapped boxes and baskets filled with Maya's handmade delicacies. The Christmas packages were in addition to the à la carte candies displayed behind the glassed-in counter. There, chocolate lovers could create their own magical mix of cordials, truffles or pieces of pure, rich chocolate. Souvenir candy shopping was exactly what Pepper had come to do before returning home to Texas. Well, she'd come to do a little Christmas shopping and to say goodbye.

Stopping to admire a towering display of holiday fudge, Pepper was overcome by doubt—was she really ready to leave St. Michel to return to Texas?

Pepper's mother, who had fled to St. Michel with her daughter, planned to stay in Europe indefinitely—at least until the furor over the scandal died down. But Pepper had grown restless. It was time to go home. Time to reclaim her life. Or at least that was what she'd told herself when she'd started out on foot that morning.

The producers of the reality television show *Catering to Dallas,* of which she was a cast member, had been wonderful about granting her a short leave as she tried to make sense of the turn of events that had landed her father in jail and sent her mother into hiding. The press had been hounding Pepper, too, and at first, St. Michel seemed like the perfect place to seek sanctuary. But as her father sat in prison—denied bail because the judge deemed him a flight risk—it hadn't taken long for the press to catch up with Pepper and her mother.

The turning point had come when her father's lawyer had relayed a message to Pepper on behalf of her father: the longer she hid away, the worse the collapse of the family's Texas Star empire made them look. In other words, the family looked guilty by sequestering themselves. Of course, that was ridiculous because neither she nor her mother had anything to do with Texas Star Energy. It was merely guilt by association. The media and the masses couldn't get to Pepper's father, Harris Merriweather. The next best thing was to flog the family members.

His attorney, Ethan Webster, had provided money for a return ticket home. Pepper had made a deal with him. She would go back to Texas, but her mother, Marjory, would remain in St. Michel. Her father was right. There was no reason she should remain in hiding.

Besides, the news of Texas Star's demise alleged internal corruption and spawned fears that thousands would suffer financial devastation from the collapse that had sent shock waves around the world.

Pepper had begun to go stir-crazy. Here, she had taken to leaving at odd hours in an attempt to dodge the paparazzi. Some mornings—like this one—it worked. Many times it didn't. She might as well hide in the comfort of her own home and try to work out a way that she could return to her place on *Catering to Dallas*. If that was possible. And if it wasn't…

The future uncertainty felt a little overwhelming, but this morning the coziness of Maya's quaint little chocolate shop felt…safe.

Still, she couldn't hide out forever. The faster she got home and resumed her normal life, the faster this nightmare would come to an end. Her father's lawyers would help him prove his innocence, and the Merriweathers' lives would return to normal—well, as normal as they'd ever been.

Since her mother insisted on remaining in St. Michel, it was Pepper's duty to set the public tone, and that began with going home.

First order of business would be to go see her father and strategize. She'd asked his main attorney, Ethan Webster, to arrange for a visit as soon as she got home. She needed to know how she could best help her father, and the best way to do that was to ask the man himself.

Even though they were in the midst of a family crisis, Pepper couldn't help feeling hopeful—that perhaps this was her opportunity to finally forge a relationship with her father.

At thirty-three years old, this might be her opportunity to set the past twenty-seven rocky years right.

Actually, the more she thought about it, *rocky* wasn't really a good description of their father-daughter relationship.

Neutral was more like it.

Detached. Disengaged. Disconnected.

Maybe now things could change.

Pepper took a deep breath, inhaling the sweet scent of cocoa and cinnamon and something…floral? Was that a hint of rose she detected? Before she could tell, the delicious notes melded into a mélange of scrumptiousness that made Pepper's mouth water…and her heart ache in peculiar, unfamiliar longing. Her hand fluttered to her chest.

What was wrong with her? This wasn't about leaving St. Michel or returning home. Was it?

Dear God, not another anxiety attack.

No, she was okay…she breathed in deeply. Sometimes the smell of chocolate worked better than Xanax.

This morning, she'd been drawn to the shop like a bee to a flower… Well, more like a chocoholic drawn to the best darn chocolate in the world.

As Maya appeared through the part in the deep cranberry-colored brocade curtains that concealed the back of the shop from the front of the house, she wiped her fingertips on a white linen tea towel.

"Ah! Bonjour, Pepper! I thought that might be you." She set the cloth on the counter, then briskly brushed her hands together, beaming a gigantic smile as radiant as the French summer sun. The simple gesture warmed Pepper from the inside out.

"Good morning!" Pepper swiped at a wisp of blond hair that the earlier gust of wind had blown out of place.

"What brings you out on this cold, blustery day, *mon amie?*" Maya stepped from behind the counter and greeted her friend with kisses on both cheeks. "Regardless, I am so happy to see you. You don't need a reason to pay me a visit. I will get you some hot chocolate to help warm you up, *oui?*"

Before Pepper could answer, the redhead had turned and was already heading to the small burner behind the case where she prepared the warm, rich beverages.

"Maya, what is that floral scent I smell in here this morning?"

Maya whipped around to look at Pepper and tilted her head to the side, a curious little grin lifting the edges of her mouth. "You can smell that?"

Pepper nodded. "Yes. It sort of smells like… roses."

Maya set down the copper bottom saucepan she was holding. "One moment, I'll be right back."

She disappeared behind the purple curtain, only to return quickly with a rectangular pink-and-black box tied with black ribbon—her shop's signature packaging.

Maya's eyes sparkled as she held it out to Pepper. "These are for you, my dear."

It was Pepper's turn to gaze at Maya curiously. "Well, thank you. Actually, I have come to purchase some chocolate. But not for myself. It's for friends. Back home." Pepper took a deep breath as she stared down at the pretty box. Finally, she squared her shoulders. "Maya, I'm leaving. I've actually come to say goodbye."

Maya responded with a resolute nod, but Pepper sensed her stoic mask hid something else. She could see a certain glint in her friend's eyes.

She shrugged it off, however, chalking it up to her own sadness and uncertainty.

"So, that means if I come home without a suitcase full of treasures from your shop, I will be run out of town on a rail." She shrugged again and a little hiccup of a laugh escaped before she could stop it. "Although others may run me out of town anyway, but I'll put up a valiant fight to stay. And possibly bribe them with chocolate."

She grimaced. Perhaps *bribe* wasn't such a good word choice since her family name was implicated in a financial scandal.

Since Pepper's father had never been to St.

Michel, the small European principality had been a good sanctuary for her and her mother. When they were here, they were surrounded by good people and good friends. They were staying with Pepper's boarding school buddy, Margeaux Broussard Lejardin, whose sister-in-law just happened to be the queen of St. Michel.

Despite the scandal, Margeaux had welcomed them with open arms, insisting they stay as long as they liked in the small two-bedroom guest cottage on the grounds of the estate where she lived with her husband, Henri.

But it was time to go home. Even Maya seemed to understand that.

"*Mon amie,* as much as I would love for you to stay in St. Michel permanently, I've said all along that you have nothing to be ashamed of, nothing to fear. You should not let narrow-minded people convict *you* for a crime *you* did not commit."

Pepper nodded, fighting the protective impulse that was bubbling up inside her, the part of her that wanted to defend her father—wanted to make sure that Maya wasn't implying that her dad was guilty. He hadn't been to trial yet, and Pepper would maintain that he was innocent until proven otherwise. But Maya had been a dear friend and because of that, Pepper checked the urge to ask the woman to clarify what she meant.

Instead, she said, "That's why it's time for me

to go. But first I need chocolate, Maya. No matter how broke a girl is, she should always treat herself to the best chocolate in the world."

Maya's smile returned. "Of course, my lovely. But before we tend to that task, I want you to take a look inside the box I just gave you."

Carefully, Pepper untied the black organza ribbon that adorned the package. As she lifted the lid, revealing a dozen white truffles dusted with dried flowers and gold dust, the unmistakable rose scent she'd smelled earlier wafted out, making her mouth water and her heart beat a little faster.

"Maya, these are beautiful. Thank you."

"You're very welcome. I made them just for *you*. A going-away present."

Pepper smiled. "But you didn't know I was leaving until just a moment ago."

The glimmer had returned to Maya's eyes again, and for a split second Pepper wondered if somehow her friend had, in fact, known before she'd told her. But that would be impossible. Wouldn't it?

"Yes, but I knew you were leaving sometime, my dear friend. Pepper, you have too much to offer. Keeping yourself locked away from the world is the crime. Let these chocolates be symbolic of everything sweet, rich and passionate that you deserve in your life. When you take the first bite of this chocolate, I want you to hold in your mind a picture of your heart's desire and then go out there and claim it for your own."

Outside, the wind resumed its ominous song, and the shop's sign danced along in perfect time. From where Pepper stood next to the window, she had a clear view of the midnight-blue placard with its crackled paint and golden lettering: Maya's Chocolates ~ Happily Ever After Starts Here.

An odd sensation coursed through her veins and she glanced down at the box in her hands, full of Maya's beautiful handiwork.

Why not?

Maya nodded. "Try one."

Pepper picked up a truffle and made a wish for her very own happily-ever-after.

Chapter Two

The flight from Paris barely made it to the gate at JFK International Airport in time for Pepper to go through customs, recheck her luggage and catch her connecting flight home. Delays leaving Charles De Gaulle Airport out of Paris had cut it dangerously close for her to catch the red-eye home. Yet, luck was on her side. She was one of the last passengers to board the plane bound for the Dallas/Fort Worth International Airport.

Once onboard, she struggled to stash her carry-on in the overhead compartment, astounded that there was still space available at this late hour. Thank goodness Ethan had purchased her a ticket in business class where the seats were generous and they weren't packed in like sardines.

The man who was sitting in the seat directly below the compartment she was claiming tossed the black cowboy hat he'd been holding on his lap onto the seat next to him, stood while doing an agile bend and dip to avoid whacking his head on the overhead console and unfolded to his full height in front of her.

"Here, let me help you with that, ma'am."

Ma'am? Only because she detected a slight Texas twang in his speech did she not take offense to him calling her *ma'am*. Instead, she chose to think, *What a gentleman.*

"Thank you," she said as she looked up into brown eyes as dark and rich as Maya's chocolates. They contrasted sharply with his spiky, sandy-blond hair. *Good-looking guy. Polite, too,* she thought.

And he was tall. Very tall. Probably six-four. The big, manly cowboy variety, with long, jean-clad legs and broad shoulders that flexed underneath his blue oxford cloth shirt as he lifted and stowed the bag in one fluid motion.

Pepper forced her gaze from the delicious show of muscles and strength, scooted past him and picked up the man's cowboy hat before she tucked herself into the seat next to the window. When she'd settled herself and glanced out the window she breathed a sigh of relief. Not only had she made the connecting flight, but she was back on U.S. soil. No one in the New York airport had hassled her. Of course, along her sprint to get from customs to her Dallas-bound flight she hadn't paused long enough for anyone to recognize her and not that anyone would in New York. But it was highly possible that anyone on board this flight might realize she was Harris Merriweather's daughter and start something.

But so far so good. Keeping her face toward the window, she heaved another sigh of relief.

It was good to be home. Or almost, anyway.

"Sorry, I'll take that from you," the male voice said.

When Pepper looked, he was motioning to the hat.

"Oh, right, here you go," she said. "And thanks again for helping me stash the suitcase."

As he accepted the hat, there was a flicker of recognition in his eyes. "No problem."

His brow furrowed, and his gaze searched her face.

Oh, no, here it comes. She braced herself.

"I'm Rob Macintyre. Have we met?"

Okay, not as bad as what she'd feared. But she needed to nip this in the bud. "No, I don't think so, but it's a pleasure meeting you now."

Her brain raced as she tried to think of a diversion, a way to change the subject without being rude or, worse yet, antagonistic.

It was only a three-hour flight from New York to Dallas, but it could feel like an eternity if things got out of hand.

Thank goodness the flight attendants began their demonstration on the hows and whys of the emergency exits and oxygen masks. Rob…what did he say his last name was? *Macintyre, right.*

Rob Macintyre… It did sound a little familiar… *Hmmm…*

Anyway, Rob Macintyre turned his attention to the safety instructions, and Pepper adjusted her seat belt and settled back into her seat.

Then it hit her—*Robert Macintyre?*

Of course. She stole another glance at him to make sure she had the right guy. With his square jaw and sculpted cheekbones, his profile was just as handsome as his face was full-on. Not only was he one of the youngest oil barons in Texas, but he was also the enigma of the Dallas social scene; at the top of everyone's guest list but always declining invitations.

No one could figure out why he was so antisocial, and that made him all the more appealing. Pepper had never met him personally—until today, and he certainly seemed anything but antisocial—but everyone in Dallas knew of him. And why not? He was young, rich, single and gorgeous.

He caught her staring and she looked away, only

to glance back a moment later to have the same thing happen again.

Pepper felt heat ignite in her décolletage and begin to trail its way up her neck to her cheeks. With hopes that he wouldn't notice, she bent down and picked up her purse, and to have something to do—and to keep herself from looking at him—she rifled through her handbag.

When she came across the box of chocolates that Maya had given her before she left St. Michel, she took it out of her purse, removed the lid and offered Rob one of the truffles. "As a thank-you for helping me with my bag," she said.

He regarded the box, then looked up at her. Suddenly, she wasn't quite sure what had compelled her to share her chocolate treasures, limited as they were. Of course, she didn't need to eat a dozen truffles, but she hadn't really planned on giving them away, either. Not until she found herself offering them to her seatmate. Oh, well, it was too late to withdraw the offer, especially after he said, "Thanks, those look delicious."

As he bit into the candy, she decided that if he did figure out who she was—the same way it had dawned on her who *he* was—at least he couldn't say she wasn't nice to him. After all, she had shared her chocolate.

Yep, when all else failed, bribe 'em with chocolate. That was definitely becoming her motto.

"I'm sorry, you'll need to stow your purse under the seat in front of you," said the flight attendant. "We will be taking off momentarily."

Pepper complied, and much to her relief, she and Robert carried on an easy, nonconfrontational conversation—talking about everything and nothing, steering clear of the personal—for the entire trip as the Boeing 757 carried them through the night from New York to the Dallas/Fort Worth airport.

After the plane landed, Robert retrieved Pepper's carry-on, setting it down for her so that all she had to do was wheel it off the plane.

"Hey, it was really nice talking to you," he said.

"It was," she agreed. "I really enjoyed it." She paused, hoping he would ask for her number, even though the last thing she needed right now was a new man in her life. But as she stared up at him as he casually stood in the aisle, leaning in toward her with his elbow braced on the back of the seat—good body language—she decided she could make exceptions for Robert Macintyre.

But he didn't ask for it. Instead, he gestured to her with his hat and said, "Take care."

Momentary disappointment washed over her, through her. But then she bucked up and reminded herself how busy she was going to be for the foreseeable future.

It was for the best.

But he was *so* darn gorgeous.

Oh, well.

She made her way off the plane and into the terminal. She just had to pick up her luggage at baggage claim, and then a taxi would take her home where she could sleep in her own bed for the first time in two weeks. If seeing Robert Macintyre again wasn't an option, that sounded like the next most heavenly prospect.

"Hey, I know you," said an unfamiliar, belligerent voice behind her.

Pepper tensed but kept walking without looking back. The voice didn't belong to Robert Macintyre. She knew that without turning around. This man sounded much gravellier and quarrelsome. The person might not even be talking to her.

Just keep walking.

But then there was a hand on her arm. "Hey, I'm talking to you."

Pepper turned around to the pig-nosed, scarlet face of a man who had to weigh at least three hundred pounds. He seemed as wide as he was tall. His breath was an alcoholic cloud, and his eyes were hooded and bloodshot. She sidestepped out of his grasp and wheeled her carry-on between them. As if that would help.

She looked around the terminal, but it was mostly empty. At this late hour the only life seemed to be the janitorial staff and other passengers who were disembarking from the flight she'd been on, and they seemed not to notice—or not to care—that the drunk man was hassling her.

"You're the daughter of that Merriweather bastard, aren't you?"

"Sir, it's late. I'm sorry, I need to go meet the person who is picking me up."

The taxi driver could wait all night, of course, but Mr. Drunk-and-Nasty didn't need to know that. Pepper turned and tried to walk away.

"I'm not finished with you," the man yelled after her. "Your daddy stole my money, little girl. Every single cent of my savings and retirement. But you were sitting up there like a princess in first class, weren't you?"

Pepper was paralyzed and nauseated. Rooted to the spot. She wanted to tell him *No, you're mistaken. It's all a big misunderstanding that will be sorted out once my father gets his day in court.* But the words wouldn't leave her throat.

"How do you sleep at night living like royalty when I may not even be able to feed my family?" The man reached out and shoved Pepper and she landed against something firm and warm. In a similar motion as he had handled her carry-on, Robert Macintyre whisked Pepper behind him and was staring down the man.

"Did you hear the lady, *sir?*" The emphasis in the

way he said *sir* was less polite and more of a power play. It helped that Robert seemed to hulk and tower over the squat man. "She needs to leave now. She has people waiting for her. It's rude to keep people waiting. So don't detain her and everything will be fine. Okay?"

The man didn't say anything else. He simply turned and staggered toward the exit and the small crowd of onlookers that had gathered after Robert had confronted the man began to disperse.

When most everyone was out of sight, Pepper started shaking, but she finally found her voice.

"Thank you for that," she said meekly. "I had really hoped there wouldn't be any trouble. But…"

She braced herself for the inevitable request for an explanation, but all Rob said was, "I will stay with you until you meet whoever is picking you up."

"Thank you, but that's not necessary. I still have to go to baggage claim. Security will be there. I should be fine. But thank you."

"I'll go with you to baggage claim. That guy seemed pretty looped. I don't want you to take a chance."

Pepper didn't refuse. How could she? So, they walked side by side through the ghost town of an airport, passing all the closed shops, restaurants and newsstands until they finally found their way to baggage claim.

Pepper was relieved when she didn't see Mr. Drunk-and-Nasty at the baggage carousel.

"He's gone," Pepper said. "I should be fine now. Good night, Mr. Macintyre."

"No, I'll wait with you until your ride is here."

She sighed, realizing the only way he was going to understand was if she told him the truth.

"I really appreciate your help. I don't know what I would've done without you back there. But I'm taking a cab home. Nobody is meeting me. I'll just go—"

"I'm happy to give you a ride home," Robert persisted. "My truck is parked in the garage."

The guy might have been a social recluse, but he certainly was relentless. Equal parts Southern gentleman and bulldog with his jaws locked, refusing to let go. And it was that slow-boiling persistence—and his gorgeous, hulking presence—that thrilled her.

He might have been at the top of everyone's invitation list, but she didn't know him and he didn't seem to know her, either. Unless it was an act. What better time to exact revenge on the daughter of the man who was at the top of everyone's most-hated list? There was no way in hell she was getting into the car with him at three o'clock in the morning.

As she wheeled her bags out to the taxi stand at ground transportation, there wasn't a cab in sight.

Dammit.

"I really appreciate your help. No offense but I don't know you, and it's three o'clock in the morning. So, I'll wait for a taxi."

He nodded. "Fair enough." But he didn't move.

"I do want you to know how grateful I am for your help."

"In that case, I suppose I'll have to wait with you until a cab comes."

At this time of night, that could take an hour. She looked around the desolate area. If he was going to kill her or hurt her he could've already made his move. The guy was twice her size and there was no one around to hear her protests. And what if he left and Mr. Drunk-and-Nasty came back? Then what?

Suddenly, taking the red-eye to save money and to avoid the crowded morning flights didn't seem like such a smart idea. And stubbornly refusing the only viable ride home seemed even dumber.

"I live in Celebration," she said. "Are you sure you're up for the drive?"

"I live not too far from Celebration myself. Come on. The car is this way."

He stopped. "You know, I don't blame you for being hesitant to get into the car with me—not after that crazy guy in the airport. And it's just the way the world is these days. I have a sister. If she were in your shoes right now, I can't say I'd want her to get in the car with some strange guy at three o'clock in the morning." He pulled his wallet out of his back pocket, opened it and handed her a business card and his cell phone.

"What's this?"

"Why don't you use my phone to call a friend or family member and tell them to expect you in no less than thirty minutes? You have my name there on the card. My cell number will register on their phone."

She must've been giving him a weird look because he shrugged and said, "Hey, it's all I've got. Unless you can think of a better idea."

He held out his driver's license for her to see and pointed to it. "See, face on the license matches the face on the man. Name on the license matches the name on the card. Feel better?"

She glanced down at the card. Sure enough, it was engraved with the name Robert Macintyre. She traced her finger over the gold-embossed Macintyre Enterprises and Macintyre Family Foundation logos. She hadn't realized the handsome, reclusive oil baron had a foundation. Though he obviously had a heart—or at least a strong protective streak. She glanced up at him...and a smokin' pair of lips that looked delicious.

She must've been more exhausted than she realized because not only was she accepting a ride home at three o'clock in the morning from a man she'd met only hours ago, but she was also fantasizing about kissing him.

She decided to dial her friend Sydney's number because Sydney was her only single friend. Her other close friends AJ and Caroline had recently met the loves of their lives and were living with their fiancés. No sense waking up two people when Sydney was still living alone.

"Hello?" Sydney's groggy voice came through the phone.

"Hi, it's Pepper. I'm so sorry to call and wake you up."

She explained the situation, and after assuring Sydney five times that she did not need her to come to the airport and pick her up, Sydney compromised by saying that she would wait for a call from Pepper saying she was safely at home, and if not she would send an entire fleet of Celebration's finest out searching for one Robert Macintyre.

Her British accent sounded so proper.

Especially when she said, "Is this *the* Robert Macintyre?"

"Yes, I do believe it is."

"Wait right there and let me come ride with you," she said breathlessly. "From pictures I've seen of him, he is positively yummy."

Pepper's gaze fell on Robert's lips again.

"I'll be sure and let you," she said.

After they found his black Range Rover, they fell into the same easy dialogue that they'd shared on the plane ride. As he drove, Pepper studied his profile. A bump on the bridge of his otherwise straight nose made his silhouette slightly imperfect, and a strong square jaw offsetting a full bottom lip made the imperfect look just right. At stoplights he would glance over at her and smile a smile that made her lose her train of thought.

Finally when they pulled up in front of her house, he settled back in his seat and let his gaze meander over her face, taking a long, unapologetic leisurely look.

"I can't thank you enough for how you handled things in the airport," she said.

"You didn't deserve that. No one deserves to be treated like that. I'm just glad I was there to help you."

All he'd wanted since the moment he'd first set eyes on her was to know how she would fit in his arms, how her lips would feel on his, how she would taste when he ravaged her mouth with his own. And he'd be damned if he was going to leave her tonight without knowing the answers to those questions.

He wasn't sure who moved first, but the next thing he knew he was kissing her.

She gasped a little when their lips first touched. The sound she made was barely perceptible—more of a shudder. Rob wondered if maybe he'd *felt* her more than he'd heard her reaction. But the important thing was she didn't pull away, she didn't break contact.

He shouldn't be doing this—for so many reasons. But she was kissing him back. He knew that, but her mouth was soft and warm and inviting. That little taste wasn't enough. It tortured and tempted him more than it satisfied. As they sat there, arms around each other, lip to lip, the feel of her urged him to lean in closer. When he did, her mouth parted and she invited him in.

Want swirled around him, as if his taking possession might bind her to him and fix everything that was broken. The taste of her—like cinnamon sugar and roses and something bright, like golden honey or sunshine—made him reel.

Robert Macintyre might have shied away from Dallas society, but he certainly hadn't fallen out of practice when it came to kissing. That was the one lucid thought Pepper had as she melted into him.

Rob made a noise deep in his throat, and desire coursed through Pepper, a yearning that only intensified the spell he'd cast on her. For a few beautiful seconds she thought she never wanted to catch her breath again. She could be perfectly content right here breathing his air for the rest of her life.

His rugged hands on her waist held her firmly but gently against him. Who would've guessed such a sturdy man could kiss so tenderly…yet with so much smoldering passion?

Then, just as naturally as they'd come together, they slowly released each other, staying forehead to forehead while the magic lingered.

"That was nice," he whispered. "You taste good, like that truffle you shared with me on the plane." He reached out and ran the pad of his thumb over her bottom lip.

He gave her one more wistful kiss, this one featherlight, before saying, "I'll walk you to the door."

Caught in the twilight between longing and lucidity, she couldn't find her tongue, but she was able to force her legs to carry her out of the truck and around to the back of the vehicle where he helped her with her luggage.

When they were standing at the door she could still taste him on her swollen lips.

"You have my card. If you ever need rescuing, you know where to find me."

Chapter Three

Two days later, Robert sat in his home office and sorted through a stack of mail. He deposited five invitations to parties he would normally have no intention of attending into a pile. But the thought of running into Pepper Merriweather made him rethink his standard *no*.

"Shall I RSVP *yes* to these for you?" asked his sister Kate. She'd been working for him since she'd graduated from the University of Texas with an MBA eighteen months ago.

And then he came to his senses. The last thing he needed was to go out searching for his Cinderella. Hadn't his divorce taught him that?

Rob answered Kate with a barely audible harrumph, which Kate seemed to intuitively understand. "Come on, Rob, I'll watch Cody for you. You need to get out."

He shot her his best leveling stare. "I have too much work to do this week to waste my time at parties thrown by people I don't even know."

Pepper might be there.

All the better reason not to go.

She shook her head. "If you went to these parties, you'd have the opportunity to meet them. Come on, you need a break. Get out and have some fun. Besides, the only reason anyone goes to these things is to work the circuit. There's a lot of money at these shindigs. You're missing out on opportunities for the Foundation."

She was right. But to him, working the shindig circuit, as Kate called it, ranked up there with shopping or an evening at the ballet. Simply put, he could think of a hundred other things he'd rather do—such as change the oil in his truck or wash Gabe, his Lab-like, Heinz 57 mixed breed. Or, most important, staying in with Cody, his five-year-old son and eating popcorn and watching *Spider-Man*—again.

"I pay *you* to schmooze for the Foundation. If you think these parties are such a missed opportunity, why don't you go in my place?" He turned away from the neat stacks of mail he'd created for Kate so she'd know what to do with them.

Next he began opening the emails that had come in since he'd taken a break to eat lunch with Cody, who had come home from kindergarten early today claiming he didn't feel well. He'd perked up once he saw his dad. Rob wondered if he should schedule a conference with his teacher. Being the only kid in his class who was in a wheelchair made things difficult. Kids could be so heartless. Downright mean. He didn't want Cody falling into the trap of having his old man fight his battles for him. But he was only in kindergarten.

Sometimes he sucked at being a single parent. But there was no questioning how much he loved his son.

"The only reason they invite me is because they want to hit me up for whatever cause they've deemed worthy this week."

It was true. And Rob did give back generously to the community through the Macintyre Family Foundation, where the recipients of charitable gifts were hand selected and well researched to make sure they fell within the guidelines of the MFF mission statement: Family, Community and Education. He had a real problem with these so-called nonprofits that spent a boatload of money to throw parties in the name of charity.

The truth was even though his corporation, Macintyre Enterprises, was worth more than a cool billion, the assets weren't liquid. Rob's money was tied up in oil rigs and other ventures that looked impressive on a balance sheet, but didn't allow for a whole lot of impulsive financial movement.

Hell, if he had the liquidity, there would be no need for his Foundation to beg for money for the most recent cause they'd taken on: partnering with Celebration Memorial Hospital to raise five million dollars to build a state-of-the-art pediatric wing onto the hospital. When Cody had been in the accident two years ago, he had to be airlifted to a hospital miles away for treatment. The boy was lucky to be alive. But that was one of the dark memories that Rob had sealed off, and he blinked it away to ensure it wouldn't escape.

Kate crossed her arms and gave an impatient huff. "These invitations are addressed to you, Rob, not me. I'm pretty sure they're nontransferable."

"Mmm-hmm," he grunted absently, opening and skimming an email about a project update that he'd been waiting for.

Even if Cody's wheelchair was a stark reminder of past mistakes, at least his boy was alive. That was all that mattered. More pressing was the fact that Cody would need at least one operation soon if there was ever going to be a chance that he'd walk again. Sadly, even with the Macintyre Family Foundation's personal commitment to raising the money to build the pediatric surgical wing, the facility wouldn't be ready for a while.

If he had the damn money in hand, he'd pay for the wing himself so it could be built now, and he wouldn't have to bother with parties and schmoozing and all the painful gyrations that went along with getting someone to do you a favor.

"Rob? Are you listening to me?"

"Not if you're still haranguing me about the parties."

"It would be good for you to get out every once in a while," she persisted.

His thoughts drifted to the kiss he'd shared with Pepper.

"How long are you going to punish yourself for something that wasn't your fault?"

He squinted at the computer screen, pointedly ignoring her, hoping Kate would take the hint and not go where this conversation seemed to be heading.

The door to his past was closed. Period. He would not revisit the events he'd permanently sealed behind it.

Instead, he allowed himself to revisit the memory of the kiss. It was a harmless memory. A good memory. Something that made him smile, no matter how fleeting and unsubstantial it was. But it was just a memory. He could relive it, but he wasn't going to try to recreate it. They each had their own set of weighty baggage. So they were both better off leaving each other alone.

Spending time with his son was something real

and concrete. Something he *wanted* to do. It certainly wasn't punishment. No, punishment would be spending the evening with people who would cross him off their guest list the second his net worth fell off the Forbes Rich Roster.

Much in the same way the Dallas social set had exiled Pepper and her family. She was the perfect example of how society would chew you up and spit you out once you'd fallen from grace. At one time she'd been at the top of everyone's guest list, too. Now she was the poster child for social pariahs. And as far as everyone knew, she'd had nothing to do with her family's fall from grace.

If he had a soft spot for spoiled debutantes, he might feel sorry for her. Although he did have to admit, she was nothing like what he might've imagined if he'd been inclined to follow the local players. She'd handled the drunk guy with grace and dignity. But then again, at three o'clock in the morning in the middle of an empty airport, who wanted to take on a guy who was three times her size? Things might've been different if she'd had her entourage in tow.

Then again, maybe her entourage had ditched her, too—

"But you *are* still going with me to the Raven Chair Affair next week?" Kate said. "Yes?"

Rob let his body fall back into his chair, away from his keyboard, and exhaled audibly. Scrubbing the heels of his palms over his eyes, he purposely softened his tone. "May I choose the 'bamboos under the fingernails' option instead?"

Kate rolled her eyes. "No, you may not. Raven Chairez could give the Foundation a lot of money. Somehow, I don't think I'm the one who could sweet-talk her." Kate raised her eyebrows at him in a knowing way. "You need to start practicing your manners. Now."

Raven Chairez was a piece of work. She was too old to still be throwing around her daddy's money. Even worse was the way she threw fits when his money didn't buy her exactly what she wanted. The only reason Rob knew this much about her was because Kate had briefed him about her. It struck him that if Pepper Merriweather was the poster child of the social pariah, then Raven Chairez was the picture of everything Rob hated about Dallas society. Plain and simple, she reminded him of his ex-wife. And when Kate had informed him that she'd heard through the grapevine that Raven Chairez was fixated on him—that he was a conquest she fully intended to make—Rob had made a point of avoiding all social situations where she might have the opportunity to corner him. Now, she was dangling the carrot of a potential hefty donation to the pediatric surgical wing.

One of the best ways to clinch that donation was by attending her Raven Chair Affair annual gala. Of course he would attend. But that didn't mean he had to pass up this opportunity to make his sister sweat.

"Please promise me when you hire your new assistant, you won't give her as hard a time as you give me over engagements like this."

"Are you kidding? That's special treatment I reserve only for you. Speaking of the new assistant, when are we beginning the interviews?"

They'd started the Foundation right after Kate had graduated with her master's. She had been the one who had built it into what it was today, laying the groundwork for partnering with Celebration Memorial to build the pediatric surgical wing. In the process, she'd also taken on the additional duties of caretaker for Cody and himself after he'd gone through a string of personal assistants who didn't work out.

With his divorce and Cody's accident, Rob had been under a lot of stress, and Kate had come to both his and her nephew's rescue.

It was time for his sister not only to separate the dual roles she'd been playing but to have a much deserved and long-overdue promotion within the Foundation. Rob had the unanimous support of the Foundation board, and it was a surprise Kate didn't know was coming.

"I've lined up several people for you to interview," she said. "But I'm not sure I've found the right person yet. So I'm still looking. In fact, I had lunch with Agnes Sherwood the other day. I asked her and a handful of other women of discerning taste to keep their ears open and let me know if they hear of someone good who is looking."

Agnes Sherwood was one of the Dallas area's most influential doyennes. She was the grand dame of the small affluent town of Celebration, Texas, and the woman had more money than the U.S. Treasury and commanded twice as much respect. She was just about ready to commit to a tidy donation for the pediatric wing but had to confer with her financial advisors.

"So it won't be long now and you'll have your own entourage following you around tending to your every whim."

He scowled at his sister, and she laughed at him in return. She knew how much he hated the concept of an entourage. Yet he couldn't help but think her word choice was ironic, given that he had just used it to describe Pepper and her lack of followers.

It was more like Pepper Merriweather, party of one. Pepper Merriweather with the rosebud mouth.

Pepper Merriweather, who'd obviously taken up residence in his head.

Chapter Four

Pepper wasn't quite sure she'd heard the man correctly. She leaned in, over the desk in the Celebrations, Inc., catering office that stood between them, and asked, "Excuse me?"

"I said, exactly how much did your father bilk out of the people who trusted him?"

Pepper blinked and glanced at the *Catering to Dallas* cameras, which were rolling, then back at the man. Her first thought was, *Oh, okay, this must be someone's idea of a joke.* A bad joke, granted, which they would edit out of the final footage. But when she smiled at the man and waited for him to smile back or give some other hint at a punch line, he didn't.

That's when her stomach fell and Pepper realized this wasn't a joke. The man was serious. She'd been set up.

Before Pepper had returned to work on the set of *Catering to Dallas,* she and the show's producers had agreed that any and all talk about her father and his case was off-limits on the show. Her father's attorney insisted that trying Harris Merriweather's case on a reality TV show could only hurt his chances for a fair trial when he got his day in court.

"Answer me!" the angry man demanded.

Pepper wanted to kick herself. How could she have been so naive to believe that the bigwigs of a reality television show that thrived on sensationalism would pass up the opportunity for the inside scoop about scandal and intrigue? Even Pepper had to acknowledge that it was fodder for good ratings.

But they'd promised.

And she'd believed them.

The producers had put the man on the shooting schedule, had him masquerade as a customer interested in a catering estimate. They'd even told Pepper they were bringing him in for a short "day in the life of Celebrations, Inc." vignette. This was to be a simple shot of her interacting with a potential customer. It was supposed to be a good way for her to ease back into the show.

But obviously the joke was on her.

Her next thought, as she glanced from the angry man to the rolling television cameras, was, *Ooh, this was not how happily-ever-after was supposed to begin.*

As the man proceeded to berate her and her father, Pepper's fight-or-flight response kicked in. She knew she had to get out of there. Without saying a word, she calmly turned around and grabbed her purse from a drawer in the filing cabinet behind her, stood and began walking to her car.

"Follow her!" hissed Bill Hines, the director of *Catering to Dallas.*

Pepper dared not glance back over her shoulder. Because if she did, she would be staring blankly into a television camera pointed at her face. She'd look like the proverbial deer caught in the headlights. Except, as she beelined for her car, she decided it was more apt to say she felt like a deer on the run at the opening of hunting season.

Thank goodness she'd gotten enough of a head start to allow her time to get into her car, lock the doors and drive away, escaping the unanswered questions that hung between Pepper and the camera crew.

Maybe she should've stayed in St. Michel. She'd only been home for three days, and already things were going haywire. She'd managed to slip back into the country unnoticed on an uneventful flight that arrived in the wee hours of the morning. Then she'd accepted a ride from a stranger who had kissed her senseless and disappeared into the ether.

Although he had told her to call him if she needed saving again. And she did. What would he do if she called?

Naah. She was perfectly capable of saving herself.

The first day back, when she'd finally opened her eyes, rested and refreshed, back in her own bed, back in Celebration, Texas, it was as if she'd awakened from a bad dream. For a very short window of time—with Robert Macintyre's kiss still fresh on her lips—everything seemed to indicate that she had, indeed, made the right decision to come home.

Pepper had expected that sense of security and *rightness* to carry over when she went back to work. She'd also hoped that somehow she'd hear from Rob again, but then she reminded herself that he didn't have her number—though he had Sydney's. She'd dialed it with his phone. He knew where she lived. If he'd wanted to see her again, he could've made the effort.

She hadn't told her girlfriends about the kiss. From this vantage point she was glad she hadn't. If she didn't tell, she could pretend that it never happened.

Which was probably for the best. Because coming fresh off that disaster, here she was, her first day back on the job, and she'd walked right into a setup.

She was beginning to sense a pattern.

It certainly wasn't the stuff that happily-ever-after was made of. At least not the happily-ever-after she'd held in her heart a few days ago in Maya's Chocolate Shop.

Before turning onto her street, she glanced into the rearview mirror to make sure no one was following her. When she was sure the coast was clear, she pressed the garage door opener and pulled, quickly pressed the button to shut the garage door behind her and killed the engine. She sat there for a few moments listening to the engine tick and sigh in the cool, quiet, dim space. The only light was the eerie yellow glow from the fixture attached to the automatic door opener.

For a moment it crossed her mind that this windowless garage might be the only place in the world where she could truly escape the perils and scrutiny of the outside world. Inside the house, there were windows and the television, which seemed to run a constant commentary of judgments and opinions about her father's presumed guilt, the family's involvement, her mother's choice to run away to St. Michel and Pepper's own choice to come home.

The beginning of a headache throbbed in her temples. She closed her eyes and pressed her fingers against the lids, but it didn't help. When she opened her eyes again, the dim garage door opener light had shut off. In the gray darkness, everything looked fuzzy and out of proportion, especially the shadows.

A voice of reason—a voice of fight—made her stare down the shadows, because that was the only way she could prove this dread that threatened to consume her was not bigger than she was. She alone had the power to expel all the shadow monsters, but that light had to come from inside her. Still, first she had to get out of the car.

As her eyes focused, she could see her running shoes sitting on the stoop leading up to the kitchen door. A set of golf clubs that she'd used only once leaned against the wall next to it. Her bike was suspended by chains from the ceiling above the clubs.

Wow, she'd taken so many things for granted before the rug had been yanked out from under her family.

A chill wound its way through her body. Despite the cool December weather, the air felt clammy and clung to her like a warning.

If she stayed here, it would essentially be her own version of house arrest. The thought made her heart feel so heavy it hurt.

She took a deep breath to calm herself and gripped the steering wheel. It felt good touching something tangible, something tactile, to ground her in reality.

Who would've thought that the garage and the

safety it provided had the potential to become her favorite room in the house?

And that thought was just pathetic.

She had to get herself out of this funk. Who better to call than Lindsay and Carlos, the show's executive producers? They hadn't been there today. Surely, they didn't know what had happened. There was no way they would've allowed it.

She took out her cell phone and dialed Carlos's number from her contacts. After four rings, the call went to voice mail.

"Dammit," she muttered under her breath, as she listened to the mailbox greeting. At the beep, she said, "Hi, Carlos, it's Pepper. We had a bit of confusion during filming today, and I need to talk to you and Lindsay about it. Please call me as soon as possible. Thanks."

Just as she was hanging up, another call was beeping in. The name AJ Sherwood-Antonelli flashed on the screen. AJ was Pepper's lifelong friend, business partner and costar on *Catering to Dallas*. Even seeing her name on the phone's screen made Pepper feel better.

"AJ, hi. I'm so glad you called."

"Hi, Pepper, what's going on? I heard there was some trouble during the shoot today."

Pepper shifted in her seat and the leather squeaked under the movement. "Well, that's putting it mildly." She told AJ about the bait and switch and the ensuing panic attack that had her bolting from the set.

Since her father's arrest, she had been prone to heart palpations and sudden gripping moments of utter panic. It didn't happen often, but when it did, it was almost like an out-of-body experience.

They always passed in due time, but as they were happening, the attacks were terrifying. She always had the most insane urge to run.

Fight-or-flight syndrome was what the doctor had called it. Obviously, she was a flier, not a fighter.

"I'm so sorry, hon. What a horrible thing to happen. Have you talked to Carlos and Lindsay about it? I just can't see them being okay with something like that."

"I called but didn't get an answer."

"Yeah, they mentioned that they'd be tied up with something. Probably sponsor-related. That's just about the only thing that would keep them incommunicado."

At least they were incommunicado for a valid reason. Not pathetically hiding out in a car parked in a garage. Besides, it was a little cold out here. When she'd run out she'd forgotten to grab her coat. As she let herself out of the car, she made a mental note to get it the next time she was at the Celebrations, Inc., office.

The thought gave her a sinking feeling.

"Hey, I left my red coat in the office," she said to

AJ. "Could you bring it home with you when you leave today? Maybe I can get it later."

She let herself into the house. It seemed eerily quiet, but the way the sun shone in through the windows lifted her spirits.

"Sure thing," AJ said. "We don't have any jobs on the schedule tonight. So, I should be home around seven. Want to come over for dinner?"

"That sounds heavenly. This weary soul could use some good food and a good friend—"

The doorbell rang. Since Pepper was standing in the hallway that led to the foyer, she saw Bill Hines, director of *Catering to Dallas,* staring back at her through the beveled glass door. Her heart pounded, and for a split second she wished she'd stayed in the garage despite the cold.

"*Ugh,* Bill is at the door," she said to AJ. "I really don't want to talk to him right now."

"Don't answer the door."

"I have to. We're staring at each other through the glass."

"Well, if you didn't let him in, it would serve him right."

"Or at least it would send him a message," Pepper said. "I've got to deal with him sometime. It might as well be now. But I swear to you, if he's come with a team of cameras. I will not be responsible for my actions."

"If he ambushes you for a second time, you'd be

within your right to deck him on grounds of self-defense. Or you can at least take comfort in knowing I will bail you out of jail."

There was a beat of silence on the line. "Umm, sorry about that," AJ said. "That was a poor word choice. What I was trying to say is that I'm here for you, but I'd better let you go before I put my other foot in my mouth."

Poor AJ. "No offense taken. You don't have to walk on eggshells with me. Besides I might very well need you to come and bail me out if Bill gets too fresh."

Pepper forced a laugh even though she was feeling anything but humorous. Especially when Bill rang the doorbell again.

Persistent little bugger. Did he think she couldn't see him? Could he not see that she was talking on the phone?

"Wish me luck," she lamented.

"Somehow I get the feeling Bill's the one who will need the luck," said AJ. "I wouldn't want to be on the receiving end of what I suspect he's about to get."

Pepper laughed again, but the humor was still absent from her voice. "Thanks, I'll see you tonight."

Cell phone still in hand, she walked to the door and opened it. Standing face-to-face with Bill, she did her best to resist the urge to throttle him.

He must have read the anger in her face because

he held up both hands. "I come in peace, Pepper. Please don't shoot."

She cocked a hand on her hip. "Is that how you've scripted this scene, Bill?"

He sighed and looked a little pale and defeated. "May I come in so we can talk?"

"Are you alone?"

"Of course I am."

Her gaze scanned the area behind him to make sure another television camera ambush wasn't waiting to rush in behind him if she let him in. Satisfied that the coast was clear, she stepped aside and motioned him into the foyer, then led the way to the living room without looking back. He took a seat on the white sofa. She perched on the edge of the love seat across from him, a cue that he shouldn't get too cozy because he wasn't staying long. A boxy wood, glass and mirrored coffee table was an ocean between them.

They sat in silence for a moment that seemed to stretch into eternity. Despite the discomfort, Pepper bided her time. She'd be dammed if she was going to speak first. To convey her displeasure, her gaze trailed up the paintings that graced the living room's white walls, to the dark wooden beams on the ceiling, over to the crystal chandelier that was reflecting the late morning sunlight. Slowly, her gaze meandered around the room, lingering on the vase of pale pink peonies she'd purchased yesterday to liven up the place. Then she eyed the ornate, limestone Baroque-style fireplace, skimmed over the stack of art books on the coffee table and finally landed on the ebony-stained wooden floorboards.

Bill must have gotten the message. "You know I was just doing my job, right, Pepper?" he finally said.

Just doing his job?

She didn't answer him. She couldn't. Her brain was at war with her heart, and she didn't know which one to listen to. Her heart was calling him all kinds of words that usually weren't part of her vocabulary—but he deserved to be called each and every ugly thing for expecting her to betray her father, for embarrassing her and forcing her to flee like a dog on the run.

But her head was telling her he was right. He *was* only doing his job. She should've known better than to plop herself down right in front of the rolling cameras of a reality television show.

Bill hadn't set her up. Sure, he may have lied by omission of the truth. But really she'd done a fine job setting herself up all by herself.

"They pay me to make *Catering to Dallas* successful." His voice sounded almost apologetic, a sharp contrast to the stern tone he'd used when he'd barked orders at the cameramen earlier that day. "The bottom line is, the story surrounding your dad is a gold mine. I have a responsibility to our sponsors to tap it for everything it's worth."

Pepper blinked at him. "Or?"

Bill shrugged. That was when Pepper noticed he was clenching his hands together so tightly that his knuckles were white. This wasn't any easier on him than it was on her.

"I was hoping you could help me figure that out," he said. "That's why I came over here. That, and to say I'm sorry for upsetting you today."

Pepper scooted onto the edge of the love seat. "Wait, I'm confused," she said. "If you've come over here to help me figure out what we're going to do, it sounds like you're giving me a choice."

Bill's brow furrowed, and at that instant Pepper knew.

"The only choice I have, Bill, is to cooperate with including my father's case as part of the story line, or leave the show. Right?"

Her heart started racing. What the heck was she going to do for money if she left the show? This was her job. Her livelihood.

"Basically." Bill's voice was soft and rueful.

For some reason, Pepper felt sorry for the man. He was in as tight a spot as she was. But there was no way she would sell out her father or herself.

She nodded and cleared her throat, hoping to steady her voice. She wasn't mad at Bill. He was simply part of the absurd reality TV machine. He was simply doing his job.

"Then I will make this very easy on both of us," she said. Her voice was gentle and she tried her best to turn up the corners of her mouth into a smile. "If you will let me out of my contract, I will resign from the show."

He unclasped his hands. Leaning forward, he opened his mouth as if he were going to say something, but ultimately clamped his lips shut and remained silent.

Pepper could read between the lines: there was no other alternative. Not unless she caved. And she certainly wasn't going to do that.

She stood. "Please let me know if we need to formalize anything. But I suppose my resignation is effective immediately."

Bill stood. "I wish you would reconsider."

Pepper took extra care to keep her tone soft. "Reconsider selling out my own father for the proverbial fifteen minutes of fame? That's not how I operate, Bill, but it's what you need for this show, and I can't help you there. I won't be the reason my father is tried and convicted before he goes to jail. Because to get the sensational television material you're looking for, it would turn out that way."

Pepper turned and began walking toward the front door. She heard Bill's footsteps behind her on the hardwood.

"If your father goes to jail it will be because he was convicted by a jury of his peers. Your bowing out of *Catering to Dallas* isn't going to change that."

She opened the door. "But my bowing out will stop at least one source of the gossip." She opened the door. "Goodbye, Bill."

Chapter Five

When Agnes Sherwood called earlier that morning and said she wanted to meet Rob for lunch to talk about making a sizable donation to the Macintyre Family Foundation, Rob cleared his schedule.

One simply did not refuse when Agnes Sherwood requested a lunch date. Especially since Rob and Kate had been trying to pin down the matriarch on her contribution to the pediatric wing since they'd announced their commitment to raise the remaining three million dollars for Celebration Memorial Hospital.

Agnes had been out of the country for a couple of months and unavailable the past few times he and

Kate had tried to schedule meetings. It was beginning to feel like avoidance. So her phone call had come as a surprise that morning. He was eager to find out why this woman who didn't make a habit of simply doing lunch, in fact, wanted to have lunch with him. Specifically *him*. She'd asked him to meet her in downtown Celebration, which was twenty minutes north of Dallas. Of course, he was happy to comply.

He hoped the answer to why she wanted to meet would be written on a piece of paper that contained a dollar sign followed by a lot of numbers.

Rob stood when the petite, elderly woman entered the dining room at Bistro St. Germaine.

Right on time.

She wore a fitted black suit with a red blouse and sturdy-looking heels. The diamonds in her ears sparkled, as did the rock on her finger when she extended her hand to Rob.

"Good afternoon, Mrs. Sherwood," he said, accepting the proffered hand.

"Yes, I suppose it is," she answered.

"So nice to see you." Rob continued to stand as the maître d' pulled out her chair and helped her settle into her place at the table.

Once seated, Agnes Sherwood sat ramrod straight. She may have been small in stature, but the presence she projected and the respect she commanded was larger than life.

She assessed him with steely ice-blue eyes, and if he didn't know better, he might think she was actually looking down her nose at him. But that was just the way Agnes Sherwood was.

He smiled at her and her air of frosty propriety seemed to warm a few degrees.

"Thank you for suggesting that we meet," he said. "It's been far too long. How have you been?"

She didn't answer him. Instead, she opened the quilted handbag with the gold chain-link strap that was still in her lap and pulled out a rectangular piece of paper. A check, which she laid facedown on the white tablecloth between them.

"I'm going to cut right to the chase," she said. "I would like to make a donation to your Foundation to help build that children's surgical wing on to the hospital. But first, I need you to do something for me."

Curiosity burned in his veins, but he knew better than to let his gaze drop from hers to the money.

"Anything you need," he said. "You name it, you've got it."

Agnes nodded. "Do you know Pepper Merriweather?"

The mention of her name kicked his pulse into high gear, and for a moment he was taken back to that night in front of her house, could smell the roses and taste the sweetness of her lips. Why, suddenly, did Pepper Merriweather seem to be lurking around every corner? Obviously, with the Texas Star issue making headline and fodder for gossip, the family's name was on most people's lips, but why suddenly did Pepper keep coming up when he'd never even seen her in person before that night on the plane?

"Pepper and I have met," he said. "Why do you ask?"

"I want you to hire her," said Agnes. "She is in need of employment and your Foundation is in need of donations. So there you have it."

What the—? Hire Pepper Merriweather—?

"Hire her to do what?" he asked.

Agnes stared at him blankly. "I beg your pardon."

Rob cleared his throat. "Sorry, but I'm not sure I understand. What exactly would I be hiring Pepper Merriweather to do?"

"To work for you." Agnes sounded exasperated, as if it took every ounce of decorum she possessed to resist calling him an idiot. "Kate told me you're in need of an assistant. She asked if I knew of anyone who would be qualified. Pepper would be perfect for the job."

Pepper Merriweather as his assistant? The image of her with her wavy blond hair and big brown eyes glancing up at him as she said goodbye to him that night after the airport—as she tried to be so assertive, yet looked so vulnerable, and had felt so wonderful in his arms—surged to the forefront of his mind.

Fallen debutante Pepper Merriweather serving as his personal assistant? Had she ever had a real job in her life? And how likely would she be open to schlepping for someone else?

That wasn't a fair assumption. After all, she'd been a lot different that night than he'd ever imagined she would be. He gave himself a mental shake, reminding himself that he'd never actually imagined what Pepper was like...until recently.

"No disrespect, ma'am, but why are you asking for this job on her behalf? Why isn't she here herself?"

Agnes frowned. She tilted her head back, a different method of looking down her aquiline nose. He'd never seen anyone actually do that before.

"I'm here because I'm the one with the check. That's why."

That much was true. She was the one with the money. And she came with a big, bad reputation of beating people to a pulp with her well-endowed pocketbook. But...

Wait—

"Does Pepper know that you're here on her behalf?"

"No. As a matter of fact, she does not." She reached out and toyed with the edge of the check. "I hope you will be discreet."

What was he supposed to say to that?

Again, the image of Pepper's beautiful face commandeered his thoughts.

Still toying with the check, Agnes softened her words. "I'm sure you've heard that the Merriweather family has fallen on hard times."

Rob nodded. "That's an unfortunate situation. But from what I understand, Pepper didn't work for Texas Star. So I would imagine she shouldn't have trouble finding employment for herself, if she tried. That is, if she even needs it."

Agnes chuckled the forced tolerance of someone in the know. "The majority of people in this town won't even speak to her, much less hire her. This unfortunate situation with her father has cost her opportunities. And, sadly, her trust was connected to Texas Star—something with the way it was taxed. But that's none of our business. Are you aware that she had been cast on that reality television show *Catering to Dallas,* along with my granddaughter, AJ Sherwood-Antonelli? AJ is the chef and owner of Celebrations, Inc., Catering. She and Pepper have been friends since primary school. Pepper is like a granddaughter to me. So naturally I wanted to help her help herself."

Rob nodded. Now Agnes's concern for Pepper was beginning to make sense. He had heard something about the television show that was being filmed locally, but since he didn't watch reality TV, it had flown under his radar.

"My granddaughter informed me that because of Pepper's family situation, she has been forced off the show. There was a short blurb about it in the latest issue of the *Dallas Journal of Business and Development*. Did you see it?"

He shook his head. Strange, he'd read all the feature stories in the paper. How did he miss it?

"Which section was it in?"

Agnes rolled her eyes. "It was in that little gossip column they run. You probably don't read that section. The only reason I know about this is because my granddaughter pointed it out. Anyhow, now she needs a job. That's where you come in."

She reached out and flipped over the check. "After you hire her I will give your Foundation this check for five hundred thousand dollars."

What the hell? Was this woman really trying to bribe him into hiring Pepper Merriweather with a Foundation donation? He knew Agnes took no prisoners when it came to issues she was passionate about, but did she really think she could manipulate him?

On one hand, the reality that she was backing him into a corner really irked him. On the other hand, five hundred thousand dollars was a big chunk of change towards the financial goal for the pediatric wing. He'd be a fool to let the donation get away. It wasn't as if she was asking him to do something illegal or as if he would benefit personally. In that regard, it would be irresponsible to let a donation of this size get away. Still, it was the principle of the matter, the way she was going about it, throwing her money at him as if she could beat him into submission, that irked him.

"So, let me get this straight. Are you saying you will withhold support of a worthy cause that will benefit the children of this community if I don't hire Pepper Merriweather?"

Agnes pursed her lips. "We do what we must, Mr. Macintyre."

"I'll be honest, Mrs. Sherwood. Your approach to this donation bothers me on so many levels—"

"I beg your—"

"Let me finish, please. One of my main concerns is that I think you're selling Pepper Merriweather short. Why not just have her come in and interview rather than buy her way in?"

Agnes's ice-blue eyes flashed. "I do not buy anyone's way in, Mr. Macintyre. I expect her to use her talents and earn her own way. This is not a purchase as much as it is an endorsement. She has hit a bump in life's road and she deserves a hand up. Once she's gotten her footing, I am confident she will find her own way. In the meantime, I'm offering your charity an immediate opportunity to help someone in need. That good gesture will in turn benefit many more once the pediatric wing is built."

Her cell phone rang and she slipped it out of her

bag and glanced at the screen. "Excuse me, Mr. Macintyre, I have to take this call."

Rob stood as Agnes excused herself from the table and walked out of earshot.

He gave his head a shake, trying to order his thoughts and not let his pride and temper—which wanted to tell the eccentric old woman exactly what she could do with her money, pressuring him this way—get in the way of what was important.

He drummed his fingers on the table. *Think. Think.*

Sadly, he couldn't shake the thought that he was mortified for Pepper. Sure, he'd only had one conversation with her, but his gut told him that she was quite capable of taking care of herself. But what had happened with the television show?

He pulled his smart phone from his jacket pocket and accessed his mobile subscription of the *Dallas Journal of Business and Development*. He'd read this week's edition, but as Agnes speculated, he'd skipped the Grapevine section. Gossip and hearsay didn't interest him. When the file loaded, he cursored over to the Grapevine section.

There was the story.

Heiress Leaves Locally Filmed Reality TV Show Insiders report that after one day back on the set of the reality television show Catering to Dallas, *local celebutante Pepper*

> *Merriweather has resigned from the not yet released show due to conflicts over her role in the program's story line. Sources close to the production say she adamantly refused to talk about her father, Harris Merriweather, or his legal woes on the show. Mr. Merriweather is CEO of the recently bankrupt Texas Star Energy empire and is currently being held without bail after a judge ruled him a flight risk. Props to Pepper for taking one for the Merriweather team. Meanwhile, sources close to the family report that Marjory Merriweather, wife of Harris, is still in hiding in Europe.*

Props to Pepper for taking one for the Merriweather team indeed. At least she was loyal.

He tucked his cell back into the breast pocket of his jacket. She had a conscience, class and a backbone, too. Exactly the type of person he'd like to have on board at Macintyre Enterprises. But would she really be open to serving as his personal assistant? And could they keep their hands off each other long enough to get any work done? Those were the burning questions.

After Agnes returned and they'd settled back into their places, Rob asked, "Are you sure she wants a job like this? The pay is probably a fraction of what she's used to, and I can be a demanding boss."

Agnes smiled victoriously. "So that means you'll hire her?"

Rob shook his head, more out of frustration than anything else. "Let's start with an interview—or better yet, a résumé."

What would be on the résumé of a debutante like Pepper Merriweather? Finding out might make this game Agnes was playing worthwhile. And of course, there was the donation.

"Very good," said Agnes. "I am sure you won't regret this, Mr. Macintyre."

"I hope not," he said, fighting the sinking feeling that he would.

Chapter Six

Mere words couldn't have explained how happy Pepper was when she received a call from AJ inviting her over that Sunday for a girls' brunch. Right now, she couldn't think of anything that would soothe her weary soul better than time with her besties, AJ, Caroline and Sydney.

Once upon a time, they had gathered weekly, enjoying countless pitchers of Bellinis and delectable culinary delights at the granite-topped island in AJ's kitchen. But that was before AJ and Caroline had met the loves of their lives, before they'd all been swept away by their involvement on the show *Catering to Dallas,* before the fall of Texas Star and

Pepper's unceremonious exit from the show had cast shadows and doubts in Pepper's mind.

In retrospect, she was furious with herself for believing that she could come out of hiding in St. Michel and put herself directly in the public eye without someone bringing up the big, shiny, blinged-out elephant in the room. That big, shiny elephant would be her father.

She was usually savvier than that. But in her haste to prove to the world that the Merriweather family was fine—that her father would soon be vindicated—she had lost sight of the harsh realities of the cold, cruel world.

Pepper adjusted her gloved hand on the handles of the big brown paper bag full of boxes of Maya's chocolate from St. Michel and knocked on the glossy, red front door of AJ's modest bungalow.

AJ had hung a festive holly wreath festooned with red berries that matched the color of the door and gold organza ribbon that swayed when the cold wind blew. There were clusters of gorgeous red and white poinsettias on the porch. The scene made Pepper want to hum "It's Beginning to Look a Lot Like Christmas." But she didn't, because with her father in jail and her mother in St. Michel, the last thing she wanted to think about was spending Christmas alone.

Earlier that day, Ethan Webster, her father's attorney, had relayed the heartbreaking message that her dad did not want to see her. The only explanation the lawyer provided was that her father had not listed any names on his visitation list and he had indicated that he didn't plan on receiving any visitors for the foreseeable future.

"Try to empathize, Ms. Merriweather," Webster had said. "Your father is a very proud man and he probably doesn't want his wife and daughter to see him this way."

Hours after they spoke, Webster's words still rang hollow and cold, numbing her, even as she reasoned with herself: her father had never been very good at thinking of others. It had always been business first. Really, there was no room for anything to come second. Especially not family. Especially not after Carson's accident.

The memory of her twin brother made the numbness go away. It was edged out by a low-grade ache that started in her soul and radiated outward, reminding her that the accident was her fault, and she would always bear that burden.

So why should it come as a surprise that her father didn't want to see her?

Moments like this left her two choices: she could either curl up in a fetal position or she could flip the switch on these memories that no penance could ever set right.

She sucked in a breath, steeled herself and noted the absence of her friends' cars. That probably meant she was the first one to arrive. It was the first time she'd be seeing everyone since she'd made the decision to leave the show. Butterflies swooped in her belly…the sensation was a far cry better than numbness. Or the ache. She blinked away the thought, refocusing on how she and the girls had talked on the phone, and how each one had been heartbreakingly supportive of her and outraged that she'd been backed into a corner that had left her no choice but to resign from the show. Still, she felt a pang of…of what? Nerves? Apprehension? Envy?

After all, the four of them had been in this business together from day one, when they'd founded and funded Celebrations, Inc., Catering, allowing AJ, a top-notch chef, to realize her dreams of breaking out of the restaurant sous-chef mire and running her own kitchen. They'd each played a role in getting the restaurant off the ground: AJ had been the chef and culinary creative force; by trade, Caroline had been a financial analyst, but at heart she was a frustrated pastry chef—and she'd left the boring world of accounting and come on full-time at the catering company to realize her sweet dreams; Sydney had initially moonlighted as Celebrations, Inc.'s very part-time marketing and public relations guru until she was laid off from Texas Star, right before its big crash, now she was with Celebrations, Inc., full-time. And Pepper had been—what she liked to refer to herself as—the social connector. Working with Sydney, she'd used her social connections to steer business to the catering company.

Then of course they'd had the great fortune to land the *Catering to Dallas* television show when the Epicurean Traveler Network decided to launch a series about the catering industry in the Dallas area. The show was a coup, which promised to put the fledgling company on the map.

Everything seemed to be looking up for the four of them. Until Texas Star exploded and blew everything sky-high.

As Pepper waited for AJ to answer the door, she realized the demise of Texas Star had made her three friends bigger assets to Celebrations, Inc. But Pepper was a liability because of her last name, which was directly associated with the financial scandal.

"Pepper, hello! Come in," said Shane Harrison, AJ's fiancé. The couple had met in September when Shane was stationed at Fort Hood. It had been love at first sight, resulting in a big, fat diamond engagement ring and plans for a Valentine's Day wedding.

"Hi, Shane." She leaned in and gave him a hug and a quick peck on the cheek.

When she pulled away, he held on to her shoulders with both hands and looked at her with brotherly concern.

"You doing okay?" he asked.

Shane was a tall, handsome guy whose blond

crew cut inexplicably made Pepper think of another tall, good-looking blond guy she'd recently met and hadn't heard a peep from.

She blinked away the thought of Robert Macintyre.

"Well, honestly, I'd be lying if I didn't say I've been better, but you know what they say…the show must go on."

She forced herself not to wince at the self-deprecating pun.

Shane shrugged and had the good grace to change the subject. "Come on in. AJ's in the kitchen. Do you mind showing yourself in? I'm actually heading out to the office to finish up some work. You girls can get as rowdy as you want."

He held the door open for her while she crossed the threshold.

"Thank you. It was good to see you, Shane."

"Good to see you, too, Pepper. You hang in there, okay?" he said, as he closed the door behind himself.

It was warm inside. There was a fire burning in the fireplace in the living room. A Christmas tree stood in front of the window, decorated with lights and an eclectic mix of traditional ornaments. On top, an angel perched with outstretched arms.

As she made her way toward the kitchen, she knew she'd be lying if she wasn't a little bit worried that somehow this new turn of events might change the dynamics of their friendship. After all, she was the odd woman out. The fact was, the three of them were continuing on the show and Pepper wasn't.

She took a deep breath and reminded herself that her girlfriends had her back. Their friendship was solid. She had to stop the negative thoughts so she didn't turn this get-together into a big pity party.

As she stepped into the kitchen, she resolved it wouldn't go that route.

"Hey, gorgeous," she drawled, infusing as much sunshine into her voice as she could muster on this cold December day. "That handsome man of yours let me in."

AJ looked up from the counter where she was putting the finishing touches on a tray of something delicious that looked like canapés and beamed at her. "Hey, yourself. *You* look fabulous!"

She dried her hands on a towel and met Pepper with a warm hug.

AJ did look gorgeous, with her sleek, chin-length bob styled to chic perfection. She wore red lipstick that matched her red apron, which had Celebrations, Inc. embroidered across the bib in bold white script. Pepper had given each of the girls matching aprons on the day they'd signed the contract for *Catering to Dallas*. The memory made a lump form in Pepper's throat.

She set the bag on the closest bar stool at the granite island. Giving herself a mental shake, she shrugged out of her coat and removed her gloves. *Chin up, buttercup.* This was *not* a pity party.

Mustering another brave smile, she rattled the paper bag. "I brought chocolate. Maya's chocolate."

"Oh, give me that bag now," AJ insisted.

Pepper rifled through the bag until she came to the box with the tag for AJ.

"Don't eat them all in one sitting," she said as she handed over the confections. "Wait, scratch that. Enjoy them in the fashion that brings you the utmost pleasure."

AJ squealed and hugged Pepper again. "It was so sweet of you to bring these back. You know how we all crave Maya's chocolates."

"Hey, I may be broke, but there are some necessities in life a girl just can't skimp on. You know, I was thinking, you all should do a segment on the show where you feature her chocolates."

"Or maybe we want to keep the secret of Maya's delicious chocolates all to ourselves." AJ laughed as she tore into the box. "Actually, that's not a bad idea."

AJ eyed the assortment and selected a truffle. She raised it to her mouth, but stopped before biting into it. "It just wouldn't be any fun without you. I don't want to make you feel any worse, but Pepper, I don't want to do this show without you."

Pepper waved her off. "That's just crazy talk and I don't want to hear you say that again." She pulled at the cuff of her sleeve. "Because it *does* make me feel bad when you talk like that. This is the chance of a lifetime for Celebrations, Inc., and if you pass it up you'll make me feel terrible. So enough. Okay?"

AJ nodded and bit into the candy. "Mmmm," she said, closing her eyes. "This is fabulous. Have a piece." She gave the box a gentle nudge toward Pepper.

"Oh, no, that's okay. These are all yours. Maya made a special batch for me. White chocolate with rose petals and edible gold dust. They were almost too pretty to eat but too delicious to pass up. That's what made me think about featuring her on *Catering to Dallas*."

"I offered to share my box," AJ said. "Did you save me one of yours?"

Pepper shook her head and her thoughts drifted to Rob Macintyre and how she'd given him one of her precious dozen. "Are you kidding? They didn't last two days once I was back in Celebration."

Not to mention the one she'd shared with Robert.

"I don't blame you one bit. I wouldn't have shared them, either." A thoughtful look passed over AJ's face and she pulled out a stool and sat down, motioning for Pepper to do the same. "Have you given any thought about what you're going to do now?"

Pepper took the remaining two boxes out of the bag, set them on the plates at the two empty places AJ had set, then took a seat. "I have no idea what

I'm going to do. But I do need to get a job because I have to do something. And I need the money. Ha! Did you ever think you'd hear me say that?"

AJ was staring down at what looked like a business card in her hands. She was holding it by the edges as if it might burn her. "All right, I don't mean to pry… Actually, I should be apologizing for my grandmother, who has refined prying to a fine art. But she wanted me to give you this."

Pepper took the card from AJ, and almost dropped it when the overhead light reflected on the gold embossing, giving Pepper a strange sense of déjà vu that crystallized into *Oh, wow* when she read the name Robert Macintyre on the card. The same gold-embossed Macintyre Enterprises and Macintyre Family Foundation logos, the same name, address and phone number engraved in bold black in the body of the card. The only thing that was different was the handwritten message on the back: *Send résumé and call for an interview.*

"What is this?" she asked, looking from the card to AJ, who looked a little embarrassed.

"Apparently, my grandmother has brokered a job for you."

A job? With Macintyre Enterprises? A sense of free-falling whooshed through Pepper. "I don't understand."

And she really didn't. She wasn't sure if she'd reacted that way because she saw Robert Macintyre's name on the card—was this his roundabout way of finally getting in touch with her almost a week later? Or was it because a job might have fallen into her lap without her even having to search for it?

What kind of a job was it? Macintyre Enterprises was a huge company. Was she supposed to send *him* the résumé? Surely not. The CEO didn't collect résumés, even if he had saved her from a drunk bully, given her an identical card and kissed her until her lips throbbed.

"Who understands my grandmother? But if she says she got you a job, you know it's true."

AJ popped the cork on the bottle of prosecco and poured it into the green glass pitcher that Pepper was sure contained peach puree. What would a girls' brunch be without the traditional Bellini toast? Only, usually they waited until they were all here before they got into the drinks.

This was as good a time as any to tell her she had already made Mr. Macintyre's acquaintance. Sydney knew, and once word got out about the job, she'd start talking about the 3:00 a.m. phone call and how Robert had given Pepper a ride home. But no one but she and Robert knew about the kiss, so she didn't have to tell *everything* she knew.

"You know, this is the weirdest thing," Pepper mused. "I sat next to Robert Macintyre on the plane home the other night."

AJ stirred the concoction in the pitcher. "You must have made quite an impression."

"Not a good one, I'm afraid." She gave AJ the concise "History of Pepper and Robert" as AJ poured two flutes full of Bellini.

"Even when you think you're at your worse, you never fail to dazzle 'em, babe. Maybe someone has a little crush?"

"I don't."

Liar.

"I wasn't talking about *you.* I meant *him.* He's the one with the crush. On you."

"He's the boss. He can't have a crush on me."

Yes, and then there was that *issue.*

"He's a billionaire, baby. He can do whatever he wants."

Pepper remembered his warm brown eyes and the way she'd felt in his arms. The way his shoulder muscles had flexed and the way he'd protected her when Mr. Drunk-and-Nasty had hassled her. And his smile when he'd told her to call if she ever needed rescuing again. The adrenaline rush whooshed again. This time it swept up the butterflies like a riptide. The sensation was so strong, she had to resist putting her hand on her stomach.

Instead, she reached out and took the Bellini that AJ offered her.

"So, should we call this a toast or a shot of liquid courage?" AJ asked.

Pepper shrugged. "Both?"

The friends clinked glasses. "Cheers!" said AJ. "To a new job. And to Robert Macintyre."

"But how exactly did this happen?" Pepper asked. "Your grandmother is the one who gave you the card to give to me?"

AJ shrugged and nodded. "That's all she said. And you know how she can be when she doesn't want to elaborate."

That was true. AJ and Agnes had recently made amends after years of AJ going against Agnes Sherwood's grain. Agnes hadn't approved of AJ's choice to go to culinary school over a traditional education at an Ivy League university. But AJ had persevered. She won her grandmother's respect after she'd successfully set up Celebrations, Inc., Catering and began building a solid reputation on her own. AJ had learned that despite her grandmother's reputation for being a stern dowager, she had a secret soft spot for helping people help themselves.

Was that what was happening here? Pepper knew if Agnes Sherwood had taken her on as her special project—as much as she hated thinking of herself as a special project—then she at least had to investigate the opportunity further. It was a matter of respect. It didn't mean she had to take the job…but she couldn't deny the thought of having a legitimate reason to set foot inside Macintyre Enterprises thrilled her to the core and unleashed the butterflies all over again.

"Hit me with another shot of liquid courage, AJ. I think I'm going to need it."

Chapter Seven

Rob received Pepper Merriweather's résumé a week after his lunch with Agnes Sherwood. That same day, his office manager, Becca, had set an appointment for her to come in for an interview.

Obviously, Pepper didn't have a problem with Agnes serving as her employment broker. The interview was today at three o'clock. Rob couldn't remember a day when the minutes had ticked away any slower.

As he sat at his desk leaning back in his leather chair reading over her résumé—again—preparing for the interview, he reminded himself not to judge. There had been a day when he would've been grateful for any means to earn an honest paycheck. Sometimes circumstances demanded that people not be choosy. Pepper had followed through and sent in the résumé, which didn't contain any formal employment experience, but it did boast a roster of volunteer positions that could've commanded salaries a lot higher than what he was prepared to pay her.

So she really wanted to work as his personal assistant?

Well, experience like this meant she was dependable and resourceful. It was worth an interview—and a chance to see her again.

Pepper had narrowed it down to two suits for the interview. She stood in her closet weighing the pros and cons of each one, holding up one and then the other as she scrutinized herself in the mirror. At least she'd invested in classics. She felt good in her clothes and that should boost her confidence, despite the fact that she'd never interviewed for a job in her life.

Well, it was about time she did. She wasn't above working for a living, especially if it helped prove that the Merriweathers didn't think they were above life's rules.

She'd prove the critics wrong—

The doorbell rang, pulling her out of her mental pep talk.

She returned the suits to the rack and made her

way into the foyer where she saw Ethan Webster through the beveled glass on the front door.

Pepper's heart raced. Maybe this was finally the good news she was waiting for. Maybe her father had finally agreed to see her.

She threw open the door. "Ethan, hello!" she said, a little too enthusiastically. "Please come in."

There was a pause that lasted a few beats too long, but he stepped inside and she closed the door.

"Hello, Ms. Merriweather."

The split second after his somber tone registered, she thought, *Oh, no, he's not here with good news.* Had something happened?

She braced herself and turned, trusting he would follow her into the living room. He did.

"Please have a seat." She motioned to the sofa. "May I get you something to drink?"

"No, thank you." Now that she could see him in the afternoon light streaming in through the windows, she noticed he looked a little ashen. She had a crazy thought that if she didn't speak that maybe the two of them could simply sit there in companionable silence. If he didn't speak, then whatever it was he had come to say wouldn't be real. Unless his words breathed life into—

"I'm sorry to be calling on you with bad news." Ethan Weber stared at his hands in his lap, then he looked up, snaring her gaze and holding it unwaveringly as he said, "Your father suffered a heart attack this afternoon. I regret to inform you that he didn't make it. I am so very sorry."

She'd known before Ethan had formed the first word—before he'd even drawn in his breath preparing to speak. She'd known what he was going to say. Even so, in the nanosecond that she'd allowed herself to fathom the nightmare, her heart denied it. It was a contradiction of logic, much in the same way that she couldn't speak, yet inside she was screaming, *No!*

"Are you okay, Ms. Merriweather?"

No!

Ethan Webster blinked rapidly and shifted in his seat. "Due to the fact that he died in prison, it will be necessary for them to perform an autopsy. In the meantime, might I suggest that you make necessary arrangements for him? He recorded his wishes in his last will and testament. I have that here for you."

Ethan stood and cleared his throat. "Are you okay, Ms. Merriweather?"

No!

Pepper nodded, even though she couldn't swallow past the stone of silence lodged in her throat.

"I'm sorry for your loss," he said, looking at her, then bowing his head. "If I may assist you in any way, please don't hesitate to call."

Macintyre Enterprises was housed in a huge twenty-five-story glass-and-chrome building in the heart of downtown Dallas. Actually, the empire wasn't simply *housed* there, Pepper realized, as she reached for the door handle. Macintyre Enterprises *owned* the building, as evidenced by the name etched into the glass of the massive front door.

Still numb from the devastating blow of her father's death, she had accepted the interview with Macintyre because it seemed like what she should do—what he would've wanted her to do.

Dammit, he wouldn't even see her when he was alive. Yet here she was still trying to please him even after he was gone.

She reframed her thoughts. Since she was still not in possession of her father's ashes, she might as well force herself to do something constructive. There was no use rescheduling the interview so she could sit and mourn. Once his body was released to the funeral home, there would be no funeral. No burial. After her bereft mother found her way home, the two of them would scatter his ashes… somewhere meaningful.

Further proof that she was a bad daughter: she had no idea what he considered somewhere meaningful.

So, here she was in limbo. Each day that ticked by without progress was another day further from securing her future. Who knew how long her father's estate would be tied up in the courts—if there would even be an estate left after the justice system

was finished. That meant it was all the more important that she secure her own future.

With a heavy heart, she stepped into the massive
glass lobby and looked up. The ceiling seemed to
stretch miles above her head. All around a green-
tinged light poured in, reflecting off the chrome
furniture, fixtures and giant fountain in the center,
which sprayed a fine mist. Great—now her hair
would frizz. Everything about the space was sleek
and cold and slightly damp. Exactly the way she felt.

She consoled herself with the thought that being
here was the right thing to do. Not only did she have
herself to support, but she would have to pay for father's cremation.

Pepper pulled the collar of her coat together at
her throat to stave off the cold that seemed to be part
of her bones now. As she smoothed her hair into
place, she spied a receptionist stationed behind a
desk over to the right in front of a bank of elevators.

That would be a good place to start, she decided.

Her black pumps clicked on the marble floors.
The sound seemed to carry and echo in the cavern-
ous space that loomed above her. When she reached
the desk, the tall, slim, attractive brunette smiled a
perfect, pearly-white smile. Whoever was in charge
of staffing cared about making a good first impression. Behind the brunette there was another sign
boasting the name Macintyre Enterprises, making

it pretty clear that Macintyre was fond of marking his territory.

From the way the receptionist regarded Pepper, it was also clear that no one got past the gatekeeper without having a reason to be there.

"May I help you?" she asked.

"I'm Pepper Merriweather. I have a three o'clock appointment with...*er*...in Mr. Macintyre's office." It suddenly hit her that she had no idea who she'd be interviewing with—or, for that matter, what type of job she was interviewing for.

Good grief. She needed to get her head in the game. Actually, grief or time to grieve was a luxury she couldn't afford right now.

The receptionist eyed her, assessing her in that way that women sized up other women. She picked up the phone—a sleek, cordless model—and dialed.

Pepper assumed she'd been called to interview for a position within the Macintyre Family Foundation. Since her degree was in art history and she didn't know a thing about oil or any of Macintyre's other holdings, the Foundation was the only thing that made sense. Especially after she'd done her research. The Foundation's mission statement of *family, community and education* were all causes for which Pepper had advocated in the past. She especially loved Macintyre's latest endeavor, partnering with Celebration Memorial to raise money to build a new pediatric surgical wing.

That cause in particular hit close to home. If there had been a hospital that offered the right treatment closer to home when her twin brother, Carson, had had his accident, maybe he would be alive today.

Pepper tried to cut herself some slack because she felt vulnerable. Still, she blinked away the maudlin thoughts because dwelling on it now wouldn't help anyone. The best thing she could do would be to get out of her own head and heart right now and do something constructive.

As the woman spoke to the person on the other end of the line, Pepper looked around and did her best to calm her nerves and focus on what was ahead of her—the interview.

Despite all the efforts to refocus on the positive, she couldn't help but wonder why in the world Robert would want to hire her? It was a legitimate question. He would probably ask her why in the interview. She'd be doing herself a disservice if she didn't have an answer. Sure, she had a proven track record in fund-raising and volunteer efforts, but since the fall of Texas Star, her name wasn't exactly golden.

Stay positive.

She decided that she would reinforce her fund-raising experience and tell Robert Macintyre exactly why he and Macintyre Enterprises couldn't do without her.

Wow them with what's right and maybe he would

forget to ask the tough questions. Right. Or delude herself into believing he would.

As she waited for the receptionist to finish on the phone, she glanced around the lobby—the green glow seemed to intensify as the sun shifted. The place reminded her of Oz's Emerald City.

Robert Macintyre had been so...accessible and down to earth on the plane. When it came down to it, though, would he prove to be more like the great and powerful Oz?

Oh, she wasn't good at this interview business— the waiting, the judging. But this was practice. Even if she didn't get this job, it would give her a chance to figure out what she would do differently next time. Number one on the "Don't Do That" list was kiss the boss before the interview.

She wouldn't have if she'd known there would be a job interview opportunity around the corner.

Liar! cried a small voice inside her, and she remembered how kissing Robert Macintyre had seemed as inevitable as the tide dancing at the whim of the moon. But that was version one of her new life. Now, as she moved into version two, it was history. She needed to make all necessary adjustments and move on in the right direction—a course that did not include an encore of the kiss, no matter how much her heart begged to differ.

Only new mistakes, she reminded herself.

Only new mistakes.

She was way out of her comfort zone right now. Still, she had no choice but to suck it up and go with it. Learn from it. She hitched her handbag up on her shoulder, adjusted her grip on her folio and then tugged at the hem of her jacket.

She loved the black pencil skirt and single-breasted black jacket she'd chosen to wear today. She pushed aside the thought that black was the color of mourning and reminded herself that the clothes felt good on her body and that should help boost her confidence.

She took a deep, calming breath and placated herself with the thought that at least Agnes Sherwood was on her side and had been even before her father's death. How about that? AJ's disapproving, formidable grandma who used to strike the fear of Godzilla in their hearts when they were growing up.

Now, it seemed, Agnes was just about the only one outside of Pepper's circle of girlfriends who was on her side. Maybe Robert Macintyre was, too? She'd find out soon enough.

The brunette hung up and smiled.

"They're expecting you," she confirmed. "Go right on up."

She handed Pepper a visitor's pass and directed her to an elevator that carried her up in a straight shot to the executive offices on the twenty-fifth floor.

The doors opened into a space where the vaguely

green-tinged glow radiated through more floor-to-ceiling windows. It must have been something in the glass that cast the green glow, Pepper decided. It was the same hue that was found in old-fashioned soda bottles. But since there was nothing old fashioned about this place, maybe it was the essence of Robert Macintyre's billions that couldn't be contained. The same decor of marble floors and chrome-accented furniture was carried out in the executive offices, where a young redhead stood waiting for Pepper.

"Ms. Merriweather?"

"Yes." As the word escaped Pepper's lips, an irreverent thought crossed her mind: what would the woman have done if Pepper had said no? Would sirens and whistles have wailed? Would a net have dropped over her head or the floor fallen out from under her feet? Somehow that didn't seem so far-fetched in this state-of-the-art house of glass that housed Macintyre Enterprises. At least the thought lightened her mood.

She wouldn't dare claim to *know* the man after a three-hour plane ride and one long, wonderful kiss, but when she'd envisioned Robert in his natural habitat, this was not what she'd pictured. Somehow, it just seemed too typical of all the other Dallas tycoons who jockeyed for power and social position.

Robert Macintyre, social recluse, was supposed to be different. Earthier, more authentic.

"Welcome, Ms. Merriweather. I'm Becca, Mr. Macintyre's office manager. We spoke on the telephone? Mr. Macintyre will be with you in a moment. In the meantime, please have a seat over there." Becca pointed to a grouping of sleek white leather-and-chrome furniture arranged in front of one of the walls of windows.

Pepper walked with extra care so that her heels did not click as they had downstairs. She took a seat in a little patch of sunshine streaming in through the windows, and for the first time in a while felt the ice in her bones begin to thaw. Maybe this was a good sign?

She opened her folio and reviewed the notes she'd taken on the Macintyre Family Foundation.

A telephone rang and Becca answered it, glancing in Pepper's direction as she listened to the voice on the other end. She hung up and walked over to Pepper.

"Mr. Macintyre will see you now. May I take your coat?"

Pepper's stomach dipped and her first thought was to hang on to her coat like a warm security blanket, a buffer between Robert and her. But despite the nerves that suddenly kicked up, she thought better of wearing it into his office.

"Yes, thank you."

Pepper allowed Becca to help her out of her coat. Then, she gathered her purse and folio with extra résumés tucked inside—just in case—and followed the redhead to Robert Merriweather's door.

He stood when she entered.

"Ms. Merriweather. It's nice to see you again. May I offer my condolences for your loss. I would've been more than happy to reschedule the interview."

She wasn't sure what unnerved her the most—the condolences or his calling her Ms. Merriweather? Really?

"Call me Pepper, please. It's nice to see you, too." She squinted at him, expecting...something, though she didn't know what. "I must say this offer for the interview came as quite a surprise."

Becca was still standing by the door. "Thank you, that will be all," he said to her.

Becca nodded and left the room. There was a pause, during which Robert seemed to study her, and Pepper wasn't quite sure whether he'd heard what she'd said before he'd dismissed Becca.

She decided to let him speak first.

"Why do you want to be my personal assistant?" he asked.

"Your *what?*"

"My personal assistant. Agnes didn't tell you the details of the job, did she?"

Whoa, whoa, whoa, rewind there, big boy. About that kiss?

Pepper crossed her legs and sat ramrod straight, purposely keeping her tone in check. "Agnes didn't tell me anything. At least not herself. She relayed a message—that you had a job for me—through her granddaughter."

Oh, no. She was afraid that she'd come off a little too high and mighty, which might be misinterpreted as angry that he was using this confusing front as a reason to see her again. Or was he? Was this real or *personal?* Okay. So, he'd said, *personal assistant...*

"Are you looking for a secretary?" she asked.

"I thought the label *secretary* was politically incorrect," he corrected.

"Well, it is, if you say it that way." She only half regretted her sharp tone.

Thank goodness Robert laughed. "Then I take it that you're not interested in the job."

"Hold on there, Mr. Macintyre. I'm confused, and I think you know why. Would you please explain?"

"Only if you'll call me Rob."

That disarmed her. Rob. Not Robert. "All right, *Rob,* please tell me more."

He pushed back in his chair and steepled his hands on his stomach, regarding her. "My personal assistant left the company several months ago. Since then, my sister, Kathryn, has been serving double duty, helping out as my assistant and growing our Foundation."

Pepper's ears pricked up at the mention of the

Foundation, but she was still waiting for him to touch on…the way he'd touched her the other night.

"Since we've committed to raising the money to fund the children's pediatric surgical wing at Celebrations Hospital, she needs to be free to focus on that. Which means I need to hire a personal assistant."

"How personal are we talking?" Pepper asked.

"Not *that kind* of personal." His words burned.

He had some nerve. Then again, she'd baited him.

"Well, I'm sure you have others to interview," she said. "I'm sure you can find someone else who will deliver the exact amount of *personal* that you're looking for, because obviously I'm not your woman."

She cringed and started gathering her things, wanting to get out of there as quickly as possible.

"No, I'd say you're my woman. Because no one else comes with a half-million-dollar incentive."

"I beg your pardon?"

He blinked, looking for a moment like he'd said the wrong thing. But he recovered quickly. "You don't know about that either, do you?"

"No, I'm sorry. I have no idea what you're talking about. Agnes is paying you to hire me?"

"I guess that's what it boils down to. Although she's not paying *me* per se. She's making a donation to the Foundation."

Pepper arched a brow at him. Trying hard not

to let it show how utterly mortified she was by this under-the-table deal. First, she'd been kissed hard and put away wanting. Now she felt as though she were being bought and sold. Even if it was all in the name of the Foundation, she didn't like being a pawn in whatever game was playing out between Robert Macintyre and Agnes Sherwood.

"And if I don't take the job, will you still get your money?"

He shrugged. "Agnes and I didn't discuss that complication."

Now her blood was beginning to boil. Not only had they figured they could buy and sell her, but they thought she was so desperate that she'd take any position sight unseen. No talk of salary. No talk of duties. She'd just take whatever they wanted to give her because they seemed to think she couldn't manage on her own.

"Wow, this is especially degrading."

"I'm sorry. I thought you knew."

"I don't want people deciding my future without first discussing it with me. I don't know the first thing about being a personal assistant. I don't take dictation. I'm not good at having people order me around. And I don't type. Well, at least not fast."

She had composed and typed up all her own correspondence for the various committees she'd chaired. She'd never had a personal assistant—even when cash flow hadn't been an issue.

"I'm sorry you were forced to take me on as a stipulation for Agnes Sherwood's donation. That's not right, either."

"I do what I have to do for the children," he said.

Good grief, he seemed so smug today, sitting there like he owned the place—well, technically, he did. He wasn't the same relaxed, jean-clad, cowboy-hat-toting protector he'd been at the airport.

This was obviously a lost cause. She shouldn't have come today. She shouldn't have come at all.

"Well, that's one thing we can agree on," she said. "The children getting the services they need is what's important. Your Foundation does good work. Actually, I came in here hopeful that the job you had for me would be there. I think we both know I would make a lousy secretary. But I do hope Agnes will donate to the pediatric wing anyway. Thank you for your time."

Her hand was on the doorknob when he said her name. She turned back toward him.

"I'm sorry that something so pleasurable has made this meeting so awkward. I wish there was something I could do to make you change your mind."

The kiss. It all came back to the kiss.

She sighed. "You see, this—this right here? This is exactly the reason companies don't want employees to get romantically involved. Because when they do and it doesn't work out, things become awkward.

Right now, I'm not sure which I regret more—that this job opportunity didn't work out or that you and I didn't."

Chapter Eight

"Are you an idiot?" Kate yelled.

Yes, he was. A first-class idiot. If that wasn't giving him too much credit.

Rob thought Kate was going to throw his freshly dry-cleaned tux at him. Frankly, he deserved it. She did pull her arm back and make a rather unladylike growling noise, but she managed to contain herself and neatly lay down the garment bag instead. He thought the incongruity was rather humorous, given that she was dressed in a blue-beaded gown, with her hair done, ready to accompany him to tonight's gala.

He laughed. "That's so ladylike, Kate."

"Aunt Katie, why are you yelling at Daddy?" asked Cody, Rob's five-year-old son. "Is he in trouble again?"

Keeping his gaze glued to the television, Rob tried not to smile as he steered the wheel that was attached to the Wii remote, which controlled the racing video game he was playing with his son.

"You're darn right he's in trouble again," Kate said. "He had the chance to hire a very important lady today, but he let her get away."

"Why did you let the nice lady get away, Daddy?"

Rob had been asking himself the same question from the moment she'd walked out the door. A strange feeling settled over him, and he shot Kate a dirty look. The virtual car he was steering crashed into a wall. GAME OVER flashed on the screen.

Story of my life.

"Now you're in tr-tr-tr-…"

When Cody got excited or overly emotional he stuttered. It had been happening since his accident, and it had been made worse when his mother walked out on him.

"It's okay, buddy, just say the words slowly. You can do it."

The boy hung his head and slapped the armrests of his wheelchair. "I—I—I. I. Want. To. Say. You're in *trouble.*" He calmed down once he got the words out.

"See, you did it, Cody!" Kate cheered.

"That's not all, Aunt Katie. I want to say he is in t-t-trouble *and* he l-l-lost."

"Yes, he did lose, Cody. *Big-time*." Kate punctuated her sentence by glaring at Rob. "Do you know what an asset Pepper Merriweather could've been to us?" she asked him.

Rob stood and stretched. "She didn't want the job, okay?"

"Well, why didn't you do a better job of selling her on it?" Kate insisted.

But what could he have said to her to make her change her mind? She obviously wasn't interested. He wouldn't force himself on her.

And that sounded so sexual he had to shake his head to clear the thought. That was exactly why everything about Pepper Merriweather bothered him.

It had been a job interview. He was a professional. So why couldn't he act like one?

"Actually she wanted *your* job," he said in an attempt to refocus and shut his sister up. "Do you want me to call her back and offer it to her?"

Kate smirked at him.

Rob sat back down and pressed the button on the remote, starting another race. "Look out, buddy, I'm going to beat you this time," he said to Cody, who laughed and laughed. Playing with his son was the only thing that calmed his edgy nerves.

"Rob, come on. Do you know what time it is?" Kate asked. "You need to get dressed. We don't want to be late. You need as much time as possible to schmooze Raven Chairez into earmarking a large donation for the hospital."

Tonight was the Raven Chair Affair—the annual gala Raven Chairez put on in the name of charity, but in reality it was a thinly veiled ode to herself. The idea was that various businesses purchased black chairs and decorated them in various themes of their choice and paired them with other goods and services to entice gala attendees to bid on the chair "packages" during a silent auction at the party.

Later, the Raven Chairez Foundation—hence the name the Raven Chair Affair—chose various charitable causes to fund with the proceeds. The event might as well have been subtitled: *The Raven Chairez LOOK AT ME, LOOK AT ME! give to charity, but LOOK BACK AT ME! Affair.*

It was taking every ounce of moral fiber he possessed to put down the Wii remote, get up off the couch and get dressed.

That was why he continued to play. Well, that and because it was great to hear his son squealing with joy as he twisted and turned the plastic steering wheel. He'd had a physical therapy session yesterday that had left him sore and cranky and unable to form a sentence without stuttering. For a while, Cody had been so out of sorts Rob thought he might have to skip tonight's gala and stay home with him. But given his animated whoops and hollers over the video game, Rob knew his son was feeling better. For that, he was grateful. Even if it meant he had to go to the party tonight.

Out of the corner of his eye he could see Kate standing there with her arms crossed, watching them.

"Why didn't you offer her a position with the Foundation if that was what she wanted?" she asked.

"You know I can't just create Foundation positions. Everything has to be approved by the board because of the 501(c)3 status."

"But she could've helped both you and me," Kate said. "Besides, where does that leave the donation from Agnes Sherwood?"

"It leaves it very up in the air," he said. "But since I did my part by offering Pepper the job, I can't see how in good conscience Agnes could withhold the donation."

"A great way to solve that would be to find a way to bring Pepper Merriweather on board."

Dressed in that tight black skirt and those high heels, she'd looked even sexier today than she had that night. He'd given up denying that he was attracted to her. So it was probably for the best that things hadn't worked out.

An employee/boss relationship spelled disaster.

Acknowledging the thought somehow knocked a little of the wind out of him, but it gave Cody the opportunity to pull ahead in the virtual race.

"Yeaaah!" the boy squealed.

"No, seriously, Rob, think about it," Kate persisted. "She has mad skills when it comes to fundraising. We could use her."

He had to give his sister credit. Or maybe he should call it "nagging points." It was what made her so good at fund-raising. When she latched on to a cause she believed in, good luck convincing her to let go. *Ha!* He never thought he'd see the day when she would fly the flag for a displaced heiress, though.

"Have you been following the news lately?" he asked without looking up from the TV. "The Merriweather name isn't exactly one you want to link with money these days—especially other people's money. It might have the opposite effect on what we're trying to accomplish. Having her work internally, out of the public eye, was one thing, but I wouldn't send her out knocking on doors in the name of the Macintyre Family Foundation."

"Personally, I think she's getting a bum rap. She didn't even work for Texas Star. Why should she be held accountable for her father's sins? All she wants is an honest job."

His sister and Agnes Sherwood agreed on that.

"She turned down the one I offered her."

"You obviously didn't do it right. Maybe I should call her and talk to her."

Rob slanted a glance at his sister, causing his car

to skid and crash, ending the game with another win for his son. He didn't always let him win, but on days like this when the boy wasn't feeling one hundred percent up to snuff, Rob figured it couldn't hurt to give him a boost. It wasn't fun being confined to a wheelchair, and they were both still adjusting to the fact that his mother had chosen to cut herself out of his life. It had been hard. It was no personal loss for Rob, except in the way it had affected his son. Any little bit of joy Rob could bring his son's way, he was going to do it.

"Maybe *you* should talk to her." Rob tossed the ball in Kate's court.

"I don't know," Kate said. "Maybe you should finish what you started and this time do it right?" She quirked a brow. The look underscored the double meaning in her words, and he had to look away.

"Daddy, are you going to finish what you started with the nice lady, or is Aunt Katie gonna have to do it for you?"

Nice, he mouthed to his sister.

In the nick of time Nadia, Rob's housekeeper, ushered in the babysitter, Jennifer, a high school girl who lived a couple of miles down the road.

Cody clapped his hands when he saw her. "M-M-M-Miss J-J-Jen!"

Rob held his breath, gauging his son's reaction to the stuttering. But he was too excited to see Jennifer to let it show if it bothered him.

"Hi, Cody. Are you going to play with me to-night?" She waved at Kate and Rob and sat down on the chair next to Cody's wheelchair.

"Yeahhh! L-l-let's race, 'kay?"

"You got it," she said.

Kate followed Rob to the hallway, where they were out of earshot of the kids and the video games.

"I don't understand why you're dragging your heels over this," she said. "If we plug her into the right place within Macintyre Enterprises and the Foundation, she could be such an asset."

"But if we get all her baggage and bad public-ity, she could be a huge liability. She's never had a job. She's used to living life on her own terms. And some of the terms have been a little racy. Have you seen those pictures of her in a swimsuit in Cabo?"

A knowing smile spread over Kate's face. "No, Rob, I haven't seen the shots of Pepper Merri-weather in a swimsuit, but obviously you have. Get dressed. We'll talk about this in the car on the way to the gala."

Chapter Nine

"I blew it," Pepper lamented to her girlfriends. She wanted to bang her head on AJ's granite island. Maybe that way she'd be able to knock some sense into herself.

AJ and Sydney looked on sympathetically, as if they were unsure what to say or do.

"Well, it wasn't entirely your fault," AJ consoled. "You have a lot on your mind right now with everything that's happening with your father. Plus, I could throttle my grandmother for not telling us the entire scope of her plan. If she had, you wouldn't have wandered in there blindly. She is still going to give him that donation. I am not letting her back out of it."

Sydney shrugged. "Honey, maybe it was too soon after getting the bad news about your father to go in for a job interview. You probably weren't yourself."

If she wasn't herself then, who was she these days? That seemed to be the million-dollar question.

"I don't know, AJ," Sydney continued. "I think you should give your grandmother more credit than that. She'll pay up."

Sydney's British accent lent her statement more credence than they might have given it if she hadn't made the ordeal sound so proper.

AJ harrumphed. "When Agnes doesn't get her way she can get pretty surly."

AJ was named after her grandmother—Agnes Jane. Much to her grandmother's consternation, she had opted to go by AJ for short. They shared not only the same name but also a particular brand of stubbornness. When they disagreed, they were like two goats locking horns. When they were in a dead-lock, sometimes it wasn't pretty.

Right now, AJ had that certain look in her blue eyes and it was making Pepper nervous.

"I'm with Sydney," said Pepper. "I trust that Agnes will make good. I do appreciate that she tried to help me, I just wish she would've clued me in so that I hadn't gone in and made such a fool of myself."

"He *is* dreamy, isn't he?" Sydney mused over the top of her wineglass.

Pepper crossed her arms over her middle, as if the gesture would warm and protect her. The truth was she'd been scared. Scared of working for Rob… as his *personal assistant?* Really? Her mind had a terrible way of wandering into ways she could assist him that had absolutely nothing to do with business, and that wasn't good. It wasn't good at all.

"There's no doubt that he's a good-looking guy—"

"Honey, he is gorgeous," Sydney corrected.

"All hunky gorgeousness aside, I would never get involved with my boss."

Now she was scared that she'd blown her chance for viable employment. She needed a job, and she regretted not taking this one.

"Good!" Sydney clapped her hands like an excited child. "More Rob for me. Honey, if you don't want him, I'll take him off your hands."

A peculiar jealous weed sprouted inside Pepper. She wanted to tell Sydney, *Not on your life, sister.* But instead, she changed the subject.

"All kidding aside," she said, looking pointedly at Sydney, "I really admire what Macintyre is doing for the hospital. I did more research on the foundation after I got home. That pediatric wing is fabulous. It's right up my alley, a project I would've volunteered for regardless of pay. It's still relatively new, and I've been so distracted by everything that's happening with my father that I hadn't heard of their partnering with Celebration Memorial. Now, in retrospect, I wish I would've taken the job as Rob Macintyre's personal assistant just for the proximity to that project."

Sydney reached out and put a hand over her friend's. "Isn't that just like you, love, always looking for a way to help others, even in the midst of your own turmoil? What will be your next step, Pepper?"

Pepper loved the way Sydney's accent turned her name into something that sounded like *Peppa*. Hearing her name roll off her friend's tongue killed all territorial traces and put a smile on her face.

"I wish I knew. I guess I will have to figure out something pretty fast. Because basically, I'm broke and so is my mother. It looks like I may be the one supporting both of us, whenever she decides to come home." Pepper pulled a face that she and her friends used to use when they were young and imitating Agnes Sherwood. "But, yes, darlings, I do realize it's in extremely poor taste to discuss one's financial woes. Do forgive me."

They all laughed at the impression.

"My grandmother should give *you* some of that money she promised to give away," AJ said.

Pepper frowned. She knew her friend meant well, but still... "Okay, there are so many things wrong with that suggestion I don't even know where to begin. But the first thing that comes to mind is something about pigs flying. If Agnes puts that money anywhere other than back into her bank account, it will go to the Macintyre Family Foundation. And if you all want to help me, help me *find* a real job—don't buy me one."

She could tell by their expressions that both AJ and Sydney understood, and she could also see the wheels in their minds turning, no doubt searching for a solution to her problem.

"While we're on the subject of buying," Sydney said, "I suppose we could buy you out of your share of Celebrations, Inc.…"

After signing on for the *Catering to Dallas* television show, Pepper and her three friends had agreed that they would reinvest all profits back into the business. Things were just taking off for Celebrations. If Pepper asked for them to buy her out, it would pose a great hardship. "That's a sweet thought, Syd, but I don't want to go that route. My stake in the business feels like the only solid thing I have left in this world. The only thing that's *mine* that isn't tainted by the scandal. If it's all right with you all, I'd just as soon keep a safe distance from Celebrations, Inc., and let it continue to bloom the way it has been growing."

Of course, she wouldn't be drawing the salary the others were getting from their work on the television show. She'd cut herself out of that when she'd resigned from it. But the girls had agreed that they would each keep the money they earned that was paid to them by the Epicurean Traveler Network. Profits from business generated by the show would be reinvested into the shop, which meant they would have to discuss whether Pepper should get an equal share of that, but that was a discussion for another day. Right now, thinking about it made her head hurt, as if she were trying to solve a math word problem.

"We could always find a way to have you do su-persecret work for us in the shop, and we could pay you on the down low," AJ said.

"That sounds supersketchy," Pepper said. "What exactly would this supersecret work entail?"

AJ sipped her drink. "I don't know yet, but I'm completely open to suggestions."

Pepper sighed. "What I really want to do is work for the Macintyre Foundation. The more I think about it, the more I realize I really admire what they're doing. Do you think I'd be crazy if I called Rob back and asked him to keep me in mind if there's a future opening?"

It suddenly hit her that even though the thought of Agnes bribing Rob to hire her had prickled— hell, it had done a major number on her self-esteem; she could get her own job and she didn't have to be bought and sold—right now, pride was the last thing Pepper could afford. Really, she needed to reframe the equation and think of it in the terms of going back in there and getting herself the job she wanted.

She would have the job she'd choose. Agnes would simply be making a nice donation to a very worthy cause.

There. That was better. It felt right. She could see it so much clearer now that she'd put some distance between herself and the hunky Rob Macintyre. True, the guy seemed to do crazy things to her thinking, but she would just have to get ahold of herself if she was going to make this work.

"So, do you think that's a completely crazy idea?" she asked.

Sydney smiled. "I'd call you completely crazy if you didn't go for it."

By the time Rob and Kate arrived at the Regency Cypress Plantation and Botanical Gardens, the Raven Chair Affair was in full swing.

The venue for the party was located about twenty miles outside of Dallas at a majestic estate that had once been a working sugar plantation in the early nineteenth century. Since then, it had been refashioned into a much-sought-after venue for parties and special occasions.

Once they'd checked in, located their table and did a quick sweep through the silent auction to look at and bid on the chair packages, the cocktail hour was over and the guests were beginning to sit down to dinner.

Rob noticed, much to his relief, that he wasn't seated at the same table as Raven Chairez.

He'd half expected, half feared to be at her table, based on the way she'd used the event as a premise to call and email him over the past two weeks. She wanted to double-check on who he was bringing (and sounded thrilled when he'd told her his date would be his sister because she was the one who was actually heading up the Macintyre Foundation); she personally ensured that beef was in fact his choice of entrée; and ran it by him to see if he thought the men would prefer mojitos or the more traditional sidecar.

"Legend has it," she cooed, "that the sidecar was born during World War I at the Ritz in Paris."

What the hell was even in a sidecar? He didn't know. "I think I'm the wrong person to ask. I don't drink." He hadn't mentioned how his father's struggle with alcoholism had taken its toll. So much so that he'd vowed not to touch the stuff, especially after his father had killed himself driving drunk and nearly taken Cody with him.

Raven Chairez didn't want to hear that. She was too preoccupied with her big party. So he'd suggested that she offer both.

Given all the phone calls she'd made to him, Rob had fully prepared himself to be seated next to her at dinner. Sometimes a guy had to man up and do things he'd rather not do for the greater good.

So it was a welcome surprise when he saw that he had been placed two tables over from Raven and the chosen ones.

He thought he would have the dinner hour to shower her with attention. Not meaning to be disingenuous, he decided he would keep it all business, not leading her to believe he was offering anything more than mutual support of their charities through a business relationship.

Speaking of business relationships…his gaze swept the room looking for Pepper Merriweather. He knew it was unlikely she'd be there, but the woman had enough moxie to do something just like that. If she waltzed in here in spite of everyone, he would be less surprised than he was at not having Raven Chairez glued to his side.

Okay, now he was just sounding like an ass. Pepper wasn't interested; thank God in heaven Raven was preoccupied with her hostess duties.

Maybe he was losing his touch. He chuckled to himself. That wouldn't be such a bad thing if it were true.

During his cursory visual sweep of the room his gaze snared on Raven. He waved, but she looked away and draped herself over the shoulder of man who looked vaguely familiar. What was his name...? Lewis...? Lawrence...? Loomis...? The name escaped him, but he'd remember later.

Raven glanced back over her shoulder at Rob and took Long—that's what it was, his name was Dr. Geoffrey Long, and he was a local plastic surgeon—by the hand and led him to the table, settling him right next to her.

Well, good for him, Rob thought, as he claimed his own seat. He relished the thought that he would be able to eat his meal in peace, but he wasn't kidding himself. This reprieve simply meant he would have to make extra effort later to pay his respects to the hostess.

That was confirmed when Kate, who had been working the crowd, took her seat and whispered, "I told you we should've been early. Your last round of video games got us removed from the head table."

He laughed because he thought Kate was kidding. "What?"

She elbowed him in the ribs. "Stop laughing. It's not funny. My friend Anne Oates is working the check-in table. She asked me what we did to make Raven mad, because about fifteen minutes before we arrived she moved us from her table to this one."

"Seriously?" He was too surprised to say much more. Did people really act like that? Silently, he answered his own question: He knew some women did. His ex-wife was a prime example. She moved people around like pawns on a chessboard, positioning them to her advantage. It had been that way from the day she'd turned up pregnant with Cody until the day she walked out on them for a situation that better suited her purposes.

Caution flares had gone off the moment he'd met Raven Chairez, and Kate had informed him that rumors were circulating that he was Raven's conquest.

He'd sensed that Raven and his ex, Miranda, were cut from the same cloth—only Miranda hadn't been born with a rich daddy the way Raven had. Miranda had to create her situation, and she'd done that by getting pregnant with his child.

Well, that lesson had taught him that he would be nobody's prize. He was not up for auction or for sale.

That must've been how Pepper Merriweather had felt when she learned that she came with a half-million-dollar employment dowry. Looking at it from this vantage point, he understood. No one liked to feel personally bought or sold. Despite the bikini shots that had been taken by the paparazzi when she was on vacation, Pepper was apparently made of more substance than he'd given her credit for.

Still, there was the matter of a potential donation to the pediatric wing from the Raven Chair Affair. As dinner and the formal addresses wound down and the dancing began, he knew he needed to try to leave things on a cordial businesslike note with Raven.

"Good evening, Raven," he said.

She whirled around and feigned surprise, as if she were seeing him for the first time that evening. "Robert Macintyre." She grabbed his hand with both of hers and leaned in, offering him her cheek, which he brushed with a chaste kiss. "How lovely to see you tonight." She was still holding on to his hand as if she had no intention of letting him get away. "Are you having a good time?"

Rob smiled. "This is quite a party you've thrown tonight. Everyone's saying you've outdone yourself. Would you do me the honor of dancing with me?"

A fire smoldered in her eyes. "I thought you'd never ask."

He led her onto the dance floor, blessing his sister's name for insisting he learn the basic box step so he wouldn't look like an awkward boy at his first middle school dance.

He and Kate had never learned these things growing up. He was grateful that his sister seemed to have an innate sense of social appropriateness and worked hard to keep him in line. Though she would never admit it, he knew she would be relieved if he found someone who could take a bit of the responsibility off her—no one liked to be tethered to her brother and nephew out of a sense of obligation. But Kate was all about family, and she had certainly proven that during the horrendous eighteen months he and Cody had been through since the accident that claimed the life of Kate and Rob's father and left Cody in a wheelchair. The doctors had said the possibility of his being able to walk again was slim to none. Then the cherry on top was Miranda's grand exodus. That made the thought of ever trusting a woman again a very murky prospect. But Rob knew his sister would not stop mothering him and Cody until Rob showed signs that he was at least open to the idea of…someone.

Through the crowd, he caught a glimpse of a slight blonde who, at a glance, looked like Pepper. The possibility that it might be her made him catch his breath. But it wasn't her. On second glance, the woman looked nothing like her.

"You're so tense." Raven massaged his back with the hand that was on his shoulder. "Are you not having fun?"

"I'm having a wonderful time," he fibbed. What was he supposed to say?

"You were so late arriving I thought you'd changed your mind about coming."

Really, he hadn't been that late. Her chastising tone grated on his patience. He decided it would be best to not say anything since, once again, he wasn't sure exactly how he was supposed to respond.

"I had originally seated you at my table." She was stroking his neck with her finger. The featherlight motion tickled, but he steeled himself and resisted the urge to shrug away. "But since you were so late,

I had to relocate you. How would it have looked if I'd had empty places at the head table?"

"I apologize. I didn't realize there was a firm check-in time."

Finally, she moved her hand away from his neck. She pulled back a little bit so that she was looking him in the eyes. "Your tardiness was disrespectful. It sent a message that you don't care about me or my charity."

Oh, no, don't start with me, lady. "Look, I'm sorry. My son wasn't feeling well, and I couldn't leave until I was sure he was okay. In fact, there was one point today when I seriously doubted whether I'd be able to come at all. For me, my son comes first."

She pursed her bloodred lips and turned her cheek to him, looking everywhere but at him. "Well, this night isn't about *you*. It's *my* night and you're not going to ruin it. Thank you for the dance. I see someone I need to talk to."

Ten minutes later Rob and Kate were outside waiting for the valet to bring around the car. Kate's lips were turned up in a plastered-on smile, which meant Rob was going to catch hell when they got in the car and out of earshot of the others who were calling it an early evening. The upbraiding would go to the tune of:

"Not one of your more stellar days, huh? First, you lose Agnes Sherwood's half a million and then you alienate Raven Chairez. Maybe it *would've* been better if I'd come by myself tonight. Maybe we need to consider drawing some serious lines between Macintyre Enterprises and the Foundation. Because at this rate we're never going to raise the money for the hospital."

He reached into his pocket to get a tip for the valet and pulled out his phone. The screen showed that he'd missed a call. Funny, he hadn't felt his phone vibrate alerting him to the call.

No wonder—the call had come in at five-thirty, probably in the midst of his getting ready for the party. It was a number he didn't recognize.

"Hi, Rob, it's Pepper Merriweather. I was following up to thank you for meeting with me today. I apologize for being caught off guard by Agnes Sherwood's...*er*...donation stipulation. The more I thought about it, the more I realize she's absolutely right. The Macintyre Family Foundation is extraordinary, I love your mission of 'family, community and education.' I have a particular soft spot for your partnership with Celebration Memorial. I realize right now, you may not have any current openings within the Foundation. But I would like to talk to you more about the position that is open. If you're still interested in me, please give me a call at your earliest convenience. Thank you."

The sound of her voice was like a breath of fresh air. It made the blood rush to his head and thrum in his ears. Yes, he was interested. She had no idea exactly how interested he was. If it wasn't so late, he'd call her right now and tell her so.

Chapter Ten

For the second time in two days, Pepper found herself standing in the Emerald City atrium of Macintyre Enterprises. The same brunette was stationed at the reception desk. This time, she greeted her by name.

"Hello, Ms. Merriweather. Mr. Macintyre is expecting you." She handed her the same visitor's pass and directed her to the same elevator. "Please go right up."

She exited the elevator into the same emerald-tinged executive floor. There, she was once again greeted by Becca, who took her coat and offered her coffee. Pepper politely refused.

As Becca ushered her into Rob's office and she found herself standing face-to-face with him, it struck her that there weren't too many times in life where you were granted a do-over.

This meeting felt like one of those rare occasions.

"So, here we are again," Rob said. He really did have a great smile. It reached all the way to his eyes. Today he didn't seem a bit smug. In fact, he seemed genuinely glad to see her.

Maybe it hadn't been all him the last time they met. She had been reeling over the news about her father. Even her friends had said she wasn't herself. Now, things felt different—and that was such a blessing.

"Yes, here we are again," she said, smiling back at him. "Thanks so much for agreeing to give this one more shot."

"Before we take this any further, I have to be very up-front with you. I don't regret kissing you. I do regret any pain or uncertainty or confusion it might have caused. My company has a strict no-fraternizing policy. I fire bosses for getting romantically involved with their subordinates. Because, to quote a very wise woman for whom I have immense respect, 'when people get involved and it doesn't work out things become awkward.' That's why I, above everyone, must follow my own rules. Are you on board with that, Pepper?"

Maybe it defeated the point, maybe it didn't, but

hearing him admit that he didn't regret the kiss made her very happy. Happy enough that she could fold away the memory and move ahead with her new life.

There was something very comforting knowing that he'd be in her life. Even if they weren't romantic, at least they would see each other. Since things had been so fleeting and impermanent these days, it was nice to know that he was indeed someone she could count on.

"I am very on board with that," she said.

She smiled, and she allowed herself to acknowledge that it was okay to harbor a crush. As long as she kept that ship safely docked in the harbor.

He smiled, too. The kind of smile that shone through to his eyes. "Why don't we go over here and sit down where we can be comfortable?" He motioned to a grouping of white furniture on the opposite side of the office over by a wall of windows that was similar to those in the outer part of the executive offices. In his office, the decor had a similar feel, but the quality was superior and, she guessed, possibly more tailored to his taste.

She followed him over. He took a seat and motioned for her to do the same. Before they began, he picked up a phone that had been resting on an end table next to his chair and dialed.

"Becca, please bring us some coffee and send in Kate whenever she has a free moment."

Hmm... If Becca was the official elevator greeter and coffee fetcher, Pepper wondered what she would be doing as a personal assistant. And this Kate he was bringing in to join them—could she be Kate Macintyre, the one in charge of the Foundation? This could be interesting.

Rob hung up and turned his gaze back to Pepper. "I guess a good place to start would be for me to tell you about the job." He paused and studied her for a moment. She could see the virtual wheels turning in his mind.

"Actually," he continued, "I've rethought the job description since you were here. I had a chance to talk to my sister, Kate."

Ah, yes, she was the right Kate.

"She seems to think you are way overqualified to serve simply as a personal assistant. I happen to agree." Overqualified? Pepper's heart sank. Then why had he called her back? "Would you have any interest in starting out in the Macintyre Enterprises side of the business and eventually moving over to the Foundation once a position becomes available? You see, the snag is that all changes within the Foundation must first be approved by the board. Even though our family name is on the letterhead, the Foundation is set up as a 501(c)3, and that means my hands are tied when it comes things like this. However, Kate and I both agree that your practical experience with nonprofits and your enthusiasm for our fund-raising partnership with the hospital make you an ideal candidate to join the team. We didn't want to let you get away."

Flattery will get you anything you want.

She bit her mental tongue and concentrated on what was important—that they didn't want her to get away. Rob Macintyre wanted her here.

It was the first time in a long time—well, at least since the collapse of Texas Star—that anyone besides Agnes and her best friends had said such a thing to her.

She wondered if she should lay all her cards out on the table and, in all fairness and in the name of full disclosure, remind him that despite her father's death the Merriweather name wasn't a favorite in the business world at the moment.

But Robert Macintyre hadn't risen to this station in the business world by being uninformed. If he had agreed to give her a second chance, it wasn't a pity date. Of course, the half-million-dollar endowment probably did sweeten the pot....

She decided a simple "Thank you, I would be honored to work for such a worthy organization" was all she needed to say.

He was looking at her in that way that made her want to squirm, but she didn't dare.

"Do you mind telling me why Celebration Hospital is so near and dear to your heart?" he asked.

"You mentioned that in the voice mail you left last night."

She should've been prepared for this question. It was only natural that he'd want to know. She decided that the best way to go was to give him the abbreviated version of the story.

Despite the smile on Pepper's face, an aura of sadness seemed to settle around her. Something in her eyes, and the way she bit her bottom lip and glanced down at her hands before she spoke suggested that this extended beyond her father's recent passing.

"I had a twin brother," she began. "He died when he was six. There was an accident and they weren't able to save him."

Oh. Robert's blood ran cold. A six-year-old boy; an accident. But Pepper's story had a tragic ending…one that he couldn't fathom. He wanted to say something, but his mouth was so dry. He wanted to comfort her. Tell her he understood—at least some of the pain her family must have felt. He also gave a sent a silent thanks to the heavens that Cody was alive. All he could manage to say out loud was a solemn "I'm sorry."

She nodded. "I've often wondered if Carson— that was my brother's name—would be alive today if they'd gotten to him sooner…if the hospital would've been better equipped… My family is from Celebration. In fact, I still live there. They had to airlift him to Dallas. It was a long time ago. And what I love about your Foundation is that you were able to get the ball rolling on something that so many have tried to do but failed. How did you do it, if you don't mind me asking?"

"Not to sound glib, but I think they thought I'd personally bankroll the project."

He knew that left the question *Why* didn't *you fund it?* hanging out in the open, but he didn't think it was appropriate to discuss that at this point. To clear the air, he said, "But I did one better. I got the community to pull together to make it happen. I guess it was just time. There's obviously a great need for a pediatric surgical wing, and if the community gets behind it, I think it can make an even greater impact than if one person buys it."

As Becca delivered the coffee and fresh blueberry muffins, the phone rang. The LCD on the receiver displayed Kate's name.

"Are you going to join us?" he asked. "Becca just brought in some coffee, and I have someone here I know you'll want to talk to."

He smiled at Pepper and was happy to see that the light had been restored to her eyes. She seemed more like herself again. He put his hand over the mouthpiece and motioned to the coffee and muffins. "Please, help yourself."

"Rob, I know you're in a meeting right now,"

Kate said. "I really hate to disturb you, but Raven Chairez is in my office." Her voice did an upturn on the word *Chairez*.

Great. He knew what was coming next.

"She would like to see you for just a moment."

He stood and walked back to his desk, out of earshot and asked in a low voice, "Does she have a check in her hot little hand?"

"No." Kate's voice sounded overly cheerful. "But that's okay. I'm sure she'll understand."

He hoped so, because he wasn't going to jump through any more hoops. Not after last night. He grabbed a folio and pen off his desk, then turned and walked back toward Pepper. His gaze dropped to the graceful curve of her crossed ankles and he immediately looked away. Ironic, wasn't it, that he'd lumped her into the same superficial debutante category as Raven, yet here she was in his office, and he was getting ready to offer her a job.

That would teach him to jump to conclusions before a person had a chance to prove herself. Raven Chairez, on the other hand, was fresh out of chances.

"Please tell her I'll call her when my meeting is finished."

Kate was silent on the other end of the line, and for a moment he wondered if she'd already hung up.

"Okay, I'll tell her," she finally said, honey dripping from her words. "Will it be about an hour?"

"Something like that. But I really wanted you to meet with Pepper before she leaves. Any chance of that?"

"Possibly," Kate said. "I'd love to talk to her."

"If not, we can arrange something."

He hung up and spent the next forty-five minutes with Pepper, discussing the particulars of her position, how she could help behind the scenes until he obtained board approval to bring her on full-time at the Foundation and her salary.

He was amazed by her candor and how she truly seemed to want what was best for the organization. She told him she was happy to work behind the scenes sharing her expertise until they were sure her coming on board was a good fit.

"Don't sell yourself short," he said. "I am perfectly aware of the situation with Texas Star. You didn't work for them. In fact, yesterday, Kate said it best—you should not be held accountable for the sins of your father."

For the first time since he'd met her, he saw her visibly relax.

"I haven't gotten where I am by taking the safe route. I take calculated risks. Right now, my money is on you." He glanced at his watch. "I guess Kate is still tied up in her meeting, but I know you have her endorsement. So, let me tell you what I'm thinking. The board will meet again in January—about a month from now." He leaned in. "I'll tell you something if you promise to keep a secret."

Pepper nodded enthusiastically. "Of course. I'm a vault."

Actually, you're more like an hourglass—

And that thought was so unbelievably inappropriate.

He cleared his throat. "Anyway, the board has decided to reward my sister with a promotion. Currently, she's the Foundation representative. They want to make her the executive director. They want to surprise her at the next board meeting. What I foresee that to mean is after her promotion, we will need to hire another Foundation rep. That would be where you might come in. But in the meantime, if you're on board with it, I can put you on Macintyre Enterprise's payroll and you can start learning the ropes. Of course, if you made the switch to the Foundation, we could negotiate salary then. Does that sound like something you'd be interested in?"

The way Pepper's eyes sparkled he couldn't tell if they were brown or green. Whatever the color, they were gorgeous.

"Absolutely, I'm interested. But are you sure hiring me before the fact—before the board even approves the position—won't somehow backfire?"

He chuckled. "I may have to get board approval for the Foundation, but they have absolutely no say in what I do at Macintyre Enterprises."

They couldn't stop me if I wanted to hire you to sit here all day just so I could look at you. But he shoved that thought behind the door in his head he'd labeled *Inappropriate*—even though the thought came from the heart, it would be insulting if he tried to use that analogy. Hadn't he just reminded her not to sell herself short? He certainly wasn't going to make her feel as though he'd done exactly that.

The woman was smart. She had a quick wit and a sharp take on life. She also happened to be incredibly beautiful.

Her looks were simply a bonus.

He stood and extended his hand. "Welcome aboard. When can you start?"

She shook his hand. "Tomorrow?"

"Great. Do you have time to stop by human resources to do the paperwork right now? That way we can get the formalities out of the way."

"Sure," she said.

They paused by his office door, and he could smell her perfume—a hint of roses and spice. She smelled so good, he had to resist the urge to lean in.

Brand me inappropriate all day long.

Now that he'd brought her on board, he would be able to put his business hat back on and be her boss.

Strictly her boss, which meant no fraternizing.

But no fraternizing didn't mean he couldn't enjoy looking at her.

He opened the door. "Becca, would you please

direct Ms. Merriweather to human resources? She
will be joining our team starting tomorrow."

"You've got to be kidding me!"

The shrill voice came from behind him and he
turned to see Raven Chairez standing with Kate.
Kate looked as if she wanted to crawl under Becca's desk.

"Robert, did I hear you correctly?" Raven asked.
"Did you just say Pepper Merriweather is going to
work for you?"

"Hello, Raven," Pepper said. "It's been a while."

Raven didn't answer. Instead, she made a sound
somewhere between a huff and a snort.

"You must have perfect hearing. That's exactly
what I said. Becca, would you please—"

"No, Becca, wait." Raven sounded as though she
were talking to a dog. "Robert, may I have a moment, please?"

She didn't wait for him to answer. She simply
walked into his office, obviously expecting him to
follow her.

"Oh, for God's sake." Did her drama ever end?

"Excuse me for one second," he said to Pepper.
"One second."

He stepped into his office and closed the door.

"Robert, what are you doing? I have no idea how
on earth this woman could be useful to you. I am
about to stop you from making the worst decision

you could possibly make. Don't hire her, Robert. Believe me, you'll thank me later."

Was this really happening? Was he caught in a living nightmare or was this just another dramatic moment courtesy of Raven Chairez?

"Thank you, but Pepper didn't list you as a reference."

"As if anyone in this town would give her a reference. She's bad news. She and her crooked family."

He frowned. "I don't agree. She's smart. She has a lot of talent, good ideas. And a lot of heart."

He knew the *heart* comment would be the kicker.

Raven looked stunned for a moment. Then her black eyes flashed and she flicked her dark hair off her shoulder. "I will not be associated with the Merriweather family. Harris Merriweather has cost so many people their livelihoods, their life savings. Robert do you not have any sympathy for the poor people who have been robbed by that family? If you hire her, you are in effect offering a personal endorsement to what they've done. You will render yourself as big a social outcast as Pepper Merriweather is."

He nodded. "Lucky for me, I don't give a damn what society thinks. I live by my gut and my conscience."

Raven laughed, a brittle, hollow sound.

"Well, I will have you know, if you hire her, your

gut and conscience will cost the Celebration Memorial pediatric wing a lot of money."

He crossed his arms and cocked his head to the side. "How much money, Raven? You've been dangling this carrot long enough. Either pay up or—"

"Or what? Or *what?*" she demanded.

Rob just shook his head. "Okay, I think we're finished here."

He reached for the doorknob, and she reached out and grabbed his hand. Her long, red nails cut into his skin. "The Raven Chairez Foundation was prepared to gift one million dollars to the pediatric wing fund. But if you hire Pepper Merriweather, we can gladly find another recipient whose values and mission are more in line with what we stand for."

"Our mission statement says we stand for 'family, community and education,'" he said. "If you don't believe in that, then maybe this isn't a good match."

He opened the door and Raven flew out of there without as much as a glance back.

The four of them—even Becca—stood in stunned silence until after the elevators had carried Raven away.

Kate was the first to speak. "Oh, my gosh, I'm so sorry."

"No." Pepper shook her head. A shaking hand flew to her mouth. "I'm sorry. You see, this is what I was afraid of. This is what you will have to deal with if you bring me on board. I can't do that to you—to the pediatric wing. I heard what she said. One million dollars, Rob? You can't turn down that kind of money. I'll go. I'll just—"

He put a hand on her arm to keep her from leaving. "Are you kidding? A reaction like that from a person like Raven is the best endorsement you could hand me."

Pepper squinted at him, obviously confused.

"You're hired," he said.

"But you can't pass up a million dollars," Pepper argued.

"Then you owe the Celebration Memorial pediatric wing a million dollars. Go out there and raise it. Ultimately, that's why I'm hiring you. Prove your worth. Prove Raven Chairez wrong."

Pepper blinked. She looked from him to Kate to Becca and back to him, as if digesting what he'd just said.

Then she nodded as if she'd finally realized the beauty of the challenge. "Well, I've already brought you five hundred thousand, from Agnes Sherwood. So, technically, I only owe you another half million. But I can do it. I'll show you. I can do that and so much more."

And that promise of *so much more* was exactly what he was counting on.

Chapter Eleven

Pepper had a job.

A bona fide, paying job, doing what she loved to do for an organization she believed in. Life finally felt as if it the clouds were clearing. It was great to have something positive and constructive to focus on.

Robert had been out of town, so she'd spent her first days on the job in the office working with Kate. Later, there might be occasions when Pepper had to travel with Rob, but today they were sticking close to the home front. Kate was bringing her to Robert's ranch so that she could familiarize herself with his home office. Kate had told her it was in an outbuilding separate from the main house, located on 125 acres in a rural unincorporated area halfway between Celebration and Dallas.

As they drove, Pepper and Kate talked like old friends. There was such an easy flow between them. Kate was doing a fabulous job with the Foundation, but she was also receptive to Pepper's ideas and suggestions.

"At lunch, I got a phone call from my friend Sydney," Pepper said. "She's one of the girls who is on that *Catering to Dallas* television show that's taping locally. She had a brilliant idea. Several months ago, before the opportunity for the television show came up—" before Texas Star collapsed, she thought, but didn't say "—we were all pitching in and helping our friend AJ get a catering business off the ground. We participated in that Taste of Celebration food festival. Remember that?"

"I do," said Kate. "I was there."

"So was I. I was at the Celebrations, Inc., Catering booth."

"I loved their food," Kate said. "In fact, I'd hoped to use them to cater events. Until they went and got famous on me. Now, I'm sure the waiting list is years long."

"Hey, I've got connections," she joked. "So just let me know."

"You seem to have a lot of good connections," Kate said, as she stopped the BMW in front of a huge wrought-iron gate and swiped a plain white card. The gate swung open to admit them. Kate drove down the long gravel driveway, the tires crunching the rocks as they rolled toward an estate in the distance.

"Anyhow, I was talking to Sydney and we were wondering whether Taste of Celebration presented the Foundation the check they promised from the proceeds of the food festival."

"They did send us a check," Kate said.

"But they didn't do a formal grip-and-grin presentation?" Pepper asked.

"No, they didn't, why?"

"Well, Sydney suggested that if they hadn't done something formal, maybe *Catering to Dallas* could work it into their show. You know, stage a big check presentation and get the action on camera. It would be a win-win-win—great publicity for the hospital, the Foundation and Taste of Celebration. What do you think?"

"I think it's a wonderful idea." As Kate tossed out ideas of how the presentation could take place, Pepper watched Robert's estate draw closer.

She wasn't sure why, but the enormity of it and its sprawling land took her by surprise. Rob, in his true essence—that unpretentious guy she'd first met on the plane—was such a down-to-earth man. Maybe that was why his penchant for mammoth buildings seemed to contradict his laid-back personality. Not that he did things in a small way. Actually, the more she learned about Rob, the more she realized he didn't skimp on anything, especially his protective love for his family. But he didn't flaunt his wealth, either. He could afford his own small airport full of jets, yet he still chose to fly commercially.

She'd asked him about that before he left on this trip to California. Even her own father had purchased a private jet right before his empire crashed around him, but then again, outrageous extravagance had been one of the biggest contributors to Texas Star's demise—even though whether or not her father was solely to blame would be decided by a judge and jury.

Rob maintained that he couldn't justify the expense of owning an aircraft. He had no problem using charter services, but owning a plane just felt like too much of a commitment.

He wasn't exactly a commitment-phobe. More like he didn't take commitment lightly. It was easy for her to say since the commitment issue didn't apply to her. Her mind flashed back to the kiss they'd shared and she ignored a vague sense of disappointment. Better to know where she stood now—and to stand on solid ground—than to have this, too, crumble around her.

Pushing aside her personal feelings, she focused on what was good and right. She admired his commitment to family, business and his charity. She'd learned through a little internet reconnaissance that Rob's family was small and no stranger to tragedy. In an interview with the *Dallas Journal of Business and Development* that was dated three years ago, he'd talked about how his mother's death when he was a teenager had set him on a path to make the most of his life. He'd said he saw how difficult the loss had been on his father and that his father had succumbed to drinking for a short period of time, but thanks to the love and support of family and Alcoholics Anonymous, he'd pulled through.

But her good friend Caroline, whose fiancé, Drew, was the editor of the *Dallas Journal of Business and Development,* told her that about two years ago, Rob had moved the Macintyre Enterprises headquarters to Dallas from South Texas, and a couple of months later Rob's father had been killed in an alcohol-related auto accident. Rob's son had been badly injured, too.

Her heart broke for Rob and for Kate. And for the son she never knew Rob had. She suspected the boy was the reason for the home office. And what about the boy's mother? Where was she? And how come the Dallas rumor mill had failed to churn up that juicy tidbit?

Now that she thought about it, it seemed that the Robert Macintyre gossip chain ended with him being a gorgeous, reclusive billionaire, who obviously guarded his and his family's privacy jealously.

Pepper had so many questions.

But she was sure she would learn the answers in due time. She certainly didn't want to barrage Kate with too many questions. Especially ones of a personal nature.

Kate steered her BMW convertible up the long drive, pointing out various features of the property.

"Those are the stables," she said. "My brother is a huge horse fan. So prepare yourself. Sometimes I think he'd rather lose himself in the barn than dress up and date. And I just realized how bad that might have sounded. My brother hasn't been himself for the past couple of years. He went through a pretty nasty divorce, and I think he's still trying to pick up the emotional pieces."

"I'm sorry to hear that," she said.

Okay. One mystery solved. Divorced and broken-hearted. No wonder he tended to be a bit reclusive. And his having a son suggested a very good motive for advocating for a pediatric wing.

Interesting.

"Do you ride?" Kate asked.

Pepper shuddered and blocked an avalanche of bad memories that would bury her if she allowed them to. She wouldn't let them.

"I used to. A long time ago, but honestly, I'm not a big horse fan anymore." Frankly, she wished she'd never set eyes on the beastly animals. If she hadn't, life would have been a lot different.

Kate parked the car in front of a massive six-car garage, next to a black Range Rover. "Looks like Rob's home," she said. "He's probably in the stables. He usually heads there first after he's been away—as long as Cody's not home. Cody is his son. I'm sure you'll meet him eventually."

She opened the door and a chill breeze blew in. "I know you're not a horse fan, but would you mind if we went out to the stables to say hello? I have some things Rob needs to sign."

It wasn't where she would have chosen to hang out, but really there was no way she could refuse, it being her third day on the job. She just wished she had known she would be stomping around a horse barn and navigating mud puddles from where it had rained yesterday. She would've dressed a lot differently...worn boots or something.

"Sure," she said. "Not a problem at all. I'm adaptable."

She hoped her red suede Christian Louboutin pumps were, too.

She pulled her cashmere scarf tighter around her neck and walked the distance to the barn with Kate. The Louboutin pumps were definitely not hiking shoes, either, she thought when they finally reached their destination. Then the task of watching where she stepped superseded the way her shoes were pinching her feet. But she did her best to keep a smile on her face and go with the flow.

* * *

When Rob turned around and saw Kate and Pepper enter the stables, the first thing he thought of was how utterly out of place and uncomfortable Pepper looked tottering around on high heels in her cream-colored suit in the middle of a dirty, dusty horse barn. The way she was backlit, she looked like an angel in white—and wickedly high red heels.

"We need to get you some boots," he murmured. "Kate, why did you drag her all the way out here dressed like that? She's going to get dirty."

"Well, hello to you, too," Kate said. "We saw your car. I need to talk to you about some things. I didn't want you to take off riding where I couldn't get hold of you."

"You know you can always reach me by cell," he countered.

"But you don't always answer," she argued.

"I do when it's important. How are you, Pepper?" he asked.

"I'm obviously very overdressed," she said.

A horse whinnied and Pepper startled. Rob had to suppress a laugh because she was jumpier than a mouse in a parade of Clydesdales. She looked like she'd be more at home in Paris or on the bow of a yacht. If he didn't know her better, he'd think she looked more the type to tote around a little dog in her purse than to muck out horse stalls.

"Come on," he said. "Let's go up to the house where it's warm…and clean."

"No, really, I'm fine," said Pepper. "We don't have to leave on my account."

"Let's go," Rob said. "I'm finished out here anyway. The grounds look a little muddy. Did it rain while I was gone?"

"It did," Kate answered. "But we needed it. Though, I hope it will be clear next Tuesday. I had Becca set a tee time for you, Norman Webber and Gene Hersch."

"Norman Webber and Gene Hersch? Golfing together?" Pepper asked.

Kate nodded. "Why? Do you know them?"

"I do." Pepper flushed. "Once upon a time, they were friends of my father. I remember him saying he would never play golf with the two of them together. Apparently, they're a combustible pair. Was this golf date important?"

Kate's brow furrowed. "I was trying to maximize Rob's time. Each one has deep pockets… Combustible, you say?"

"I don't mean to butt in," Pepper said. "I just thought you should know."

Kate shot Rob a glance that suggested she'd just been handed the keys to the kingdom, a *See, I told you she was good* look. "You are so *not* butting in. This is fabulous information. When we get inside you'll have to tell me everything you know about who to pair and who not to. How do you know all this?"

"One of the perks of growing up here. Really, Dallas and Celebration are just big little towns."

"How do you feel about getting out of this big little town for a few days, Pepper?" Rob asked. "A business trip," he added quickly. "Tomorrow, actually."

Their gazes snared, and he knew she was thinking about the last time they'd flown together. Hell, he was, too, and he needed to stop that. He looked away. Kate had no idea about the kiss, and he wasn't about to have her catching on now—or ever, for that matter.

"Of course," she said, all business. "Where are we going?"

He stole a glance at her lips. *Oh, the places we could go if circumstance hadn't grounded us.*

"We're going to Disney World. Well, Orlando, actually. This morning, I was able to schedule a meeting with a group of venture capitalists. I had to move fast. So, we need to fly in tomorrow. I'll need your help with logistics once we get there. Becca is in the process of making the travel arrangements. It'll just be a quick trip—just a couple of days—but I need to make sure every moment counts."

As they approached the driveway, Nadia, Rob's housekeeper, drove up in her van.

Rob looked at his watch. Was it really that late

already? Cody was home from school. It threw him a little off-kilter. He wasn't sure he was ready for Cody to meet Pepper. Not that it should have mattered, but Rob had always done his best to keep his work and home lives separate.

Since Miranda had left and he'd won full custody of their son, he'd made a personal rule to limit Cody's exposure to his business associates. If Pepper worked out the way Rob hoped she would, then it was inevitable that she and Cody would meet. But this was happening so fast. Faster than he'd intended. Well, it was too late now.

Nadia was already lowering the chairlift with Cody on it.

"D-D-Daddy!" Cody cheered. Even though the boy stuttered through the excitement, it didn't seem to dampen his enthusiasm over Rob's return.

Rob hugged his son. "How've you been, buddy? I missed you."

As Cody answered, he felt Pepper's gaze on them. He couldn't quite peg why he was so nervous about introducing Cody to her. But sometimes when people saw that Cody was in a wheelchair, they changed. They tensed up, or talked down to him, or sent out a nervous vibe that he always picked up on.

But Pepper knew how to handle herself. She was made of good stuff—even if she didn't seem very comfortable around horses. There was no reason he shouldn't introduce her.

Kate gave the boy a quick squeeze and then began getting the report of Cody's day from Nadia.

Rob bent down, face-to-face with his son. "I want you to meet someone, bud. This is Pepper Merriweather. Ms. Merriweather is working with your aunt Katie and me. Will you say hi to her?"

Pepper walked up to Cody's wheelchair and knelt down so that she, too, was eye to eye with the boy.

"Hey, Cody, I'm Pepper. I know your dad introduced me as Ms. Merriweather, but if it's all right with him, you can just call me Pepper."

That's when Rob noticed that the hem of Pepper's angel-cream-colored skirt was dangling in a mud puddle, wicking up the muck.

He motioned to it. "I'm sorry, here—" His knees cracked as he stood and offered her his hand. But she waved it way. Instead, she just tucked the hem up underneath her and continued to converse with Cody.

Okay, so she wasn't as big a priss as he'd thought her to be in the barn.

She asked him about his day and if he had any homework.

"I'm only f-f-five," Cody said. "We don't g-g-get homework in kindergarten. But I think it would be cool if we got some."

Even though he was stuttering—and only a little bit, actually—Cody seemed perfectly at ease around

Pepper, not self-conscious or retreating into his shell like he was so prone to do around new people.

"What book do you have there?" she asked, pointing to the one tucked into the side of his wheelchair.

"*W-W-W-Where The Wild Things Are.*" He picked it up and studied it.

"The night Max wore his wolf suit…" Pepper whispered.

Rob did a double take. He laughed. What in the world was she talking about?

Cody's jaw dropped in awed amazement. "You l-l-like this book, too?"

"One of my favorites," Pepper said. "In fact, my brother used to have a wolf suit when he was about your age."

Cody's eyes got as big as two blue moons. "Did he ever have a w-w-w-wild *wumpus?*"

"All the time," Pepper said.

"Oh, can we have one sometime?" Cody asked. Not stuttering once.

"That would be so much fun," Pepper said.

"Would you read me the book now so we can plan our wild *wumpus?*" he asked earnestly.

"You know what, buddy, not right now. Miss Pepper has to leave on a trip tomorrow, and she probably has a lot to do to get ready. I'll bet Nadia would read to you if you asked her nicely."

"W-w-w-would you read it to m-m-me sometime?" he enunciated, and Rob could tell he was getting tired.

"Absolutely," Pepper replied. "It was really nice to meet you, Cody. I hope to see you again soon. You start planning the wild rumpus, will you?"

Cody nodded with gusto. "Can I w-w-w-wear a w-w-wolf suit like M-M-Max?"

"I'll see what I can do about that," she said.

Red flags went up, and he had to bite his tongue to keep from telling her not to make promises she couldn't keep. But maybe she was sincere— Anyhow, Cody wouldn't let her forget. The thought of watching highbrow Pepper Merriweather throw a wild rumpus just might be worth taking a chance.

"D-D-Daddy? Is Pepper that nice lady that you said you needed to finish what you started with her? 'C-C-Cause if not, I think you could start something with her."

Chapter Twelve

"It's too bad we couldn't bring Cody to Orlando, I'll bet he'd love Disney World," Pepper said as she stared out at the Epcot globe from the balcony of Rob's hotel suite. "Has he ever been?"

She looked back into the room. The sheers billowed in the warm Florida breeze blowing in through the open sliding doors. Through them she could see a silhouette of Rob sitting at the desk writing.

It was good to have this time away. It felt like a calm before the storm of her mother's return, which would happen after they got back from Orlando. Marjory would be home for Christmas. Pepper knew that should be a good thing. Thank goodness she still had time to work herself into that frame of mind.

To take her mind off that conundrum, she'd been wondering just what Cody was talking about when he'd asked if Pepper was the nice lady that his daddy was talking about when he said he needed to finish that thing he'd started.

Rob saw her watching him, closed his folio and joined her on the balcony.

"He hasn't been," Rob said. "Because of his accident, the poor little guy hasn't had a chance to do a lot of the things a normal five-year-old would do. I hate that."

She and Rob stood side by side, leaning against the railing. Their hands were so close, if she slid her hand an inch to the right, they would be touching.

Would that be considered finishing what he started? He had left her feeling very unfinished that night they'd met.

She glanced at their hands again.

Tempting. So very tempting.

But so very off-limits.

Aside from one incident of some whispering and pointing at the airport—"Look, that's Pepper Merriweather, Harris Merriweather's daughter. I wonder where she's jetting off to now? Spending other people's money"—the flight that morning had been uneventful. They'd had an easy flow of conversation on the plane, reminiscent of their flight home from New York, but the talk had been all business. And that was fine.

"What happened," she asked. "To Cody, I mean. If you don't mind me asking."

It was personal territory, she knew, but the words had fallen out of her mouth before she could stop them, and she wanted to know. She cared. What was wrong with that?

Rob stared straight ahead in the direction of the silver Epcot ball, which seemed to glow electric as it reflected the setting sun. He drew in a breath and exhaled, as if expelling the weight of the world.

"I left him alone with his mother, who in turn let my father take him for the day. My father wasn't supposed to be driving because he'd lost his license for driving under the influence. He chose that day not only to get sauced, but to also take my son out for a drive. They'd been to Target. The police found the bags in the car. He'd bought Cody a toy truck. That's probably what they went there for. I never knew for sure because my dad died at the scene. Ran a red light and it was all over. Just like that. Cody seems to have no memory of the accident. Other than the fact that he's in a wheelchair."

"Does he ever ask why?"

Rob shook his head.

"He will when he's ready to know," she said. "He's a smart kid, resilient."

Rob slid his hand next to hers, stroked her pinkie with his. The gentle touch took her breath away.

"I don't know if I can do this," he said.

She caught her breath and held it, until he finished his thought.

"I don't know if I can solely be your boss, Pepper. You're the first woman in a long time who's made me feel this way." He put his hand on top of hers.

His nearness made her senses ping. "Then why are you fighting it?"

"What if it doesn't work? What if I bring you into my son's life and *we* don't work?"

"You better than anyone know that there are no guarantees. You're pretty fearless when it comes to business. Still, you're cautious when it gets too close to home. I can't blame you. But I want you to know that I would never purposely hurt you or your son. Has that happened before? Other women have broken his heart?"

"His mother did."

Again she held her breath waiting for this piece of the puzzle.

"His mom couldn't handle the aftermath of the accident. She freaked out. She blamed me, my father, everyone but herself for leaving Cody with my dad. She was having an affair and would leave Cody with my dad for a few hours two or three times a week. It had been going on for a while, and I had no idea until the accident."

"Your dad didn't tell you?"

Rob shook his head. "Because of his drinking problem, Miranda and I had agreed that he shouldn't be alone with Cody. Not with him being so young—he was three years old. A kid that age needs constant supervision. Miranda wasn't working. But she still said she needed a nanny. I thought that was ridiculous and I told her so. She was his mother. She was supposed to look after him. That was her job. But she had her sights set on bigger aspirations. I wasn't refined enough for her. I was too controlling with the money. She had a long list of my faults. And in retrospect, I guess she was right."

He paused and swallowed hard. Pepper stared down at his hand on top of hers and tried to discern whether he was still in love with his ex-wife. Maybe that was where the hesitation stemmed from.

"You see, she and I came from meager roots compared to this." He gestured with his free hand, but didn't move the other from Pepper's.

"High school sweethearts?" she asked.

"Not really. I was the boy from the wrong side of the tracks. She was the girl who wanted more. We connected at a homecoming event seven years ago. I was the hometown boy who'd made it, and I was there to present a scholarship. She was the girl I could never get, and suddenly she was interested. Nine months later Cody was born. Somewhere in there I married her."

"You make it sound so romantic," Pepper said.

"I'm sorry to be a realist, but in retrospect it wasn't. Miranda saw an opportunity and she took it. She left Cody and me for a better opportunity. Nothing romantic about that."

So that explains it, she thought. "Is that why you're not really into the whole social networking gig?"

He furrowed his brow, as if he'd never really thought about it before.

"Maybe. Probably. That and because of my dad's drinking problem. When I was growing up we weren't a real social family. We didn't have a lot. Sometimes we didn't even have enough to make the electric bill. Do you know what it's like to live in a dark house? No clue when you'll get your next meal? That's why I guess I'm a little cautious with the money. I worked hard to get everything I have, but even now, somehow, this doesn't seem real to me. Like any day I might wake up and it will all be gone."

That hit home. "It's the scariest feeling in the world," Pepper said. "I'm living that right now. Until two months ago, I didn't have a financial care in the world. Then one day I woke up and my father was in jail, my mom was in hiding and almost everything else I'd known was gone."

They both stood silent for a long time, the parallelism of their lives echoing around them. Once upon a time she'd had it all; once upon a nightmare he'd had nothing. Now their roles were reversed, and the common denominator between them was they both knew all the trappings of money still didn't buy what was most important.

"I'm not looking for someone to support me," she said. Her voice was soft. The words weren't a defense as much as they were a gentle declaration of her independence. "I am scared to death, but there's something exhilarating and empowering about proving that I can stand on my own two feet."

His stare was bold and assessed her shamelessly. "That's what I've loved about you from the day I met you."

His words resonated in her soul and they offered to sweep her away. But she wouldn't allow herself to take him literally. People used the word *love* far too casually these days. This man whose hand was holding hers, invading her senses, pulling her into his arms, wasn't even sure what kind of relationship he wanted with her. Or did he? Because there they were, on the balcony of this gorgeous resort, and as his lips brushed hers again, it was as if they were the only two people in the world.

Unspoken feelings spilled over into the wordless confession of a kiss that affected her all the way down to the core of her being. Places inside her she'd been trying to ignore since the night they'd first kissed in front of her house sparked again, and this time they ignited into a blaze.

He kissed her so thoroughly that she forgot her words…her perfectly logical reasons for not mixing business with pleasure. Or maybe she no longer cared. All she knew was that all the reasons *why not* were shifting and misting around the edges, and her fears were being transported outside of herself until all that was left was the longing for this man, a longing that had taken root in her soul.

His tongue sent shivers of desire rippling through her, and her body demanded more. She wanted to smash through the walls he'd built around himself and find the real him, the man who needed and wanted and loved. She wanted to bridge the distance and reach the essence of Rob that was hidden behind all the barriers he'd erected to protect himself.

She wanted to prove to him that he had nothing to fear from her. She wasn't like the others. He didn't have to be guarded with her. As if reading her mind, his arms tightened around her, encircling her with an intimacy she realized she'd longed for her entire life.

Or maybe it was Rob that she'd been waiting for all her life? This man who shied away from getting emotionally involved. This man who had built barriers around himself out of self-preservation and protection his son. But now he seemed to be letting her in, and the magnitude of what was happening was sweeping her away to sweet places she'd only dreamed of.

Rob groaned softly, and Pepper tried to remember just how long it had been since she'd last tasted a man who overwhelmed her senses the way he did. Someone who made her crave his touch, hunger for his kiss. Someone who made her want nothing less than to be naked with him in bed for long hours until they knew each other so well they were etched in each other's hearts. All she needed was Rob. When was the last time she'd needed someone so badly— She abruptly pulled away, breaking the kiss and blinking in shock.

What the heck was she doing?

Rob stared at her wordlessly. And the magnitude of what she wanted to do weighed down on her.

He was her *boss*. She needed this job. The last thing she needed right now was to get involved with *him*. Love always complicated things. It made her vulnerable and exposed her heart to a world of potential hurt. Her life was already messed up badly enough. She didn't need to complicate things more.

She resisted the urge to touch her lips. "We should make it an early evening."

She hadn't meant to sound so abrupt. And judging from the look on Rob's face, she'd surprised him, too.

She cleared her throat. "I think we both need to get a good night's sleep. Our meeting is at eight o'clock in the morning. I'll meet you in the lobby at seven-thirty. Okay?"

Somewhere in the haze between longing and lust, Rob found what was left of his shredded senses. He gazed into Pepper's eyes, trying to understand what she was saying.

At first, all he could comprehend was that her sweet lips were only a breath away. But then he remembered something about meetings or meeting in the lobby…right…at seven-thirty in the morning.

He stood there breathless for a moment and closed his eyes, trying to gather himself. Damn, he needed to get out of there before they did something they'd both regret in the morning.

"Come on, I'll walk you back to your room," he finally said.

But Pepper wavered. The expression on her face was at odds with the words that had stopped their kiss. Was that disappointment he saw behind her Mona Lisa mask? He couldn't quite read her.

Boundaries should be a no-brainer in a boss-employee relationship. But right now the only place he wanted to be her boss was in the bedroom.

He took her by the hand and led her back into the suite. But then she reached for him and he stepped forward her to meet her halfway, taking her into his arms again.

"What do you want to do?" he whispered.

She answered him by sliding her arms around his neck, and kissing him. It was a deep, openmouthed kiss that had her fisting her hands into his shirt, pulling their bodies closer.

That was all he needed to know.

Together, they would cross the line from coworkers to lovers.

She knew she didn't want him to stop, so she kissed him and he kissed her back. She leaned into him as if her next breath depended on his.

He tasted like blackberries and cinnamon from the gum he'd been chewing earlier that day, and something exotic—that indefinable flavor that was uniquely his. Something, she suddenly realized, she'd been desperately hungering for—no, she'd been ravenous for it. For that hint of the familiar with a taste of the forbidden.

He slipped his hands between them. His fingers lingered on her stomach, slipped underneath her blouse and worked their way up to her breasts. She melted at the feel of his touch.

He slid his hands around her back and pulled her tight against him. She felt the hardness of him and was swept away in the rush of sexual fantasy.

He kissed her neck. Her head lolled to the side in approving bliss, as spirals of desire and fiery need unfurled in her belly.

"I've wanted this since that first day I saw you,"

he whispered. Nuzzling her neck, he kissed it and worked his way around to her lips. There, he kissed her with a slow and burning passion that held promises of what was to come next.

He'd never felt such overwhelming longing in his entire life. He wanted to show her how much he'd ached for her, how much he'd craved this moment. He wanted to show her with his lips and hands and body why they would be so right together.

Right there in the living room of the suite, he touched her, and in response his own body swelled and hardened. He loved the feel of her curves, so strong, yet so pliable to his touch. When he moved his hands to her hips, cupping her bottom and pulling her closer, she arched against him, firing his rigid desire.

He raised his hands to her breasts, cupping them through her white linen blouse, savoring their full curves before teasing her hard nipples. She gasped and seemed to lose herself in his touch.

The thought of making love to her caused a hungry shudder to rack his whole body. But that was nothing compared to the feel of her hand on the front of his trousers. She teased his erection through the layers of his trousers and boxers. The sensation was almost more than he could bear. Suddenly, he needed her naked so that he could bury himself inside of her.

He led her into the bedroom, eased her down, kissing her throat, her jaw, her cheeks, and tenderly biting down on her earlobe.

It felt like the first time again. He wanted to savor the moment. Slowing down, he undid each button on her blouse. In one swift, gentle motion, he lifted her so that he could remove it. Slowly, he unhooked the front clasp of her bra. He freed her breasts and lowered his head, suckling until she cried out in pleasure.

The sexy sound almost undid him.

She must have sensed as much, because she unbuttoned his trousers and slid down the zipper. He moved so that she could push his pants and boxers down. They dropped to the floor, freeing him.

She lay beneath him, looking like the most beautiful woman in the world. Had he been crazy to think he could resist her?

Then, as they lay together naked, despite the need driving him to the brink of madness, he slowed down, one more time, savoring the way her beautiful body looked and reveling in how much he wanted her.

Body to body.

Skin to skin.

Hands exploring.

Souls merging.

And then they were kissing each other deeply again, tongues thrusting, hungrily devouring each other. When he was sure she was ready, he buried himself inside her. That was when he knew without a doubt that this was where he wanted to be, where he needed to be. Always.

"Somebody made the news," Kate said.

She quirked a brow at him and slid a copy of the *National Tattler* onto his desk. "Working hard there, buddy?"

Rob stared at the grainy, black-and-white tabloid photo and the headline Fallen Heiress's Resort Love Nest. It was them, or was it? The quality of the photo was terrible. But he knew in his heart of hearts it was them as they kissed on the hotel balcony in Orlando. Good God, who had taken their picture? He hadn't even seen anyone with a camera. Not that he'd been looking.

He wondered if Pepper had seen the story. Probably not, since she hadn't called him.

The only consolation was that even though it was a front-page story, it was small. The barely legible photo and cryptic headline were below the fold of the weekly tabloid and would probably be hidden on the newsstand display racks or tucked away underneath where people wouldn't see it.

While they'd made the news, they weren't the main attraction. The general population wouldn't care. It was those who were close to him that he was concerned about—Pepper, Kate and Cody.

"Why didn't you tell me?" she asked.

"I don't tell you everything and really, this is nobody's business. We don't owe anyone an explanation."

Mainly because he didn't quite know how to explain this. He and Pepper were still in that no-man's-land of not knowing exactly what was between them. Not that he should have to defend himself.

"We are consenting adults," he said. "I don't quiz you about your love life."

"Fair enough," she said. "But there are bound to be questions and rumors. So, you might want to think up something a little smarter sounding because people are going to ask."

She sighed. "Look, I'm not upset. It just caught me off guard. I wish I didn't have to find out like this that you two have been seeing each other. I wish you'd trusted me enough to confide in me, because really I think you two would make the perfect couple."

"We didn't plan this. The Orlando trip wasn't a romantic getaway. It was business. Things... happened."

Kate's eyes got big.

His conscience nudged him. "It wasn't our first kiss."

"Really?" He couldn't read her expression, and that worried him.

"No. Pepper and I have had a strange kind of magnetic attraction since the night we met."

"And when was that? I thought you'd not met her before the interview?"

"I never said that." He told her about the night after they'd met on the flight back from New York. "But when I hired her we both agreed we would keep the relationship platonic. Obviously, that's easier said than done. She and I are still trying to figure this out. So, what were we supposed to say to others? Please don't hold this against her, okay?"

Kate's face softened. "Of course I won't, as long as you promise me something?"

He nodded. "What?"

"I want you to be true to yourself for once. For so many years you've been looking out for everyone else. Maybe this time is your time. Think about it."

Chapter Thirteen

Nothing like a tabloid story to put the pressure on an undefined relationship. Especially on the eve of her mother's return to Texas. Her mother was such a stickler for all that was proper and in good taste. If her mother had seen the photo, Pepper knew she would be hearing about how it was bad form to be caught in a romantic romp so soon after her father's passing.

After all, one must observe Victorian mourning customs. Pepper flinched at her own impertinence. Was this how things would be now that her mother was coming back?

Not necessarily. But it was important that she

set the tone. Somehow, she had to be respectful of her mother's position, while not sacrificing herself. Now that she knew where she stood with Rob, she wanted to nurture that relationship. Somehow she would have to make her mother understand that just because she was moving on with her life she was not being disrespectful of her father.

More than anything, she needed to gently make her mother understand that things were different now. That they were in survival mode and no longer had the luxury of playing to society.

The time she'd spent with Rob was a sanctuary in the storm of uncertainty. While the purest part of her longed to lose herself in him, in the new direction their relationship had turned, she couldn't ignore the niggling voice that warned her to be practical. Not to the tune of Victorian mourning customs, but to be careful. Jobs like this didn't come along every day. She needed to take extra care to remain professional and so indispensable to the Macintyre Family Foundation that if things didn't last with Rob she wouldn't find herself back at square one.

Not that she was forecasting gloom and doom. She wanted him more than was good for her. After all, she only need to take one look at her mother to see the moral of the tale of a woman who invested everything she had in a relationship.

Look where Marjory Merriweather was today.

To that end, Pepper needed to do a little damage control. She had been mortified when Rob had called the morning after they'd gotten home from Orlando and broke the news about the story. She hadn't even seen the paper. A news clipping service that Macintyre Enterprises employed to gather stories about the company had sent it to him, Rob had said.

"My take is unless someone within the organization read the tabloids and chose to make an issue of it, it won't be a problem."

"And will it become a problem if someone does raise a stink?"

Robert's answer was short and succinct: "I'm the one who signs the checks. If they don't like it they can work for someone else."

Well, that was good to know…for now. She hoped he would never have reason to take that stance with her in the future. Just to be sure—

"Where does that leave us?" she asked. He'd answered the question with silence. She wasn't comfortable with that answer. "Rob, I happen to love my job. I don't want *this*—whatever it is that's going on between us—to change things. But I also don't want to be a liability. You need to decide if I'm worth it."

Oh, gosh, did I really said that?

But it was the million-dollar question. The fact remained that she did draw a certain interest from the press—even if it was B-roll, below-the-fold gossip. To some degree, her life had always played out in the public eye. Rob, on the other hand, was a very private person.

"Of course you're worth it. I don't want to lose you, but even more than that, I want you to be comfortable in your position here."

"So, what does that mean?" she asked.

"It means that we have to keep our eyes open for the damn paparazzi."

She laughed and decided to take it as a positive. She needed to bolster herself as much as possible before facing Kate. Rob had told her that Kate *understood,* but her feelings had been hurt finding out the way she did. "Just talk to her. I think you'll be pleasantly surprised."

One of the best ways she knew to bolster herself was by giving herself a good dose of chocolate. She pulled out a piece of the mass-produced chocolate from the secret stash she kept in her pantry.

She was out of the good stuff that Maya had sent home with her. Being on a budget, she'd gone with the next best alternative. While nothing compared to Maya's chocolate, this stuff did the trick in a pinch.

She unwrapped the red foil paper, smoothed it flat and read the inspirational quote inside: *Today, have no limits.*

These little gems usually made her smile, but today's went against the grain. It should've been more to the tune of *Today is a day to set boundaries with the media*.

Pepper balled up the wrapper and sent it sailing toward the garbage can with a flick of the wrist. It landed with a soft *plunk*.

So much for that.

She decided that she would face Kate the same way she'd faced all the other challenges that had landed on her doorstep lately: head-on.

They were scheduled to meet on the set of the taping of *Catering to Dallas* for the presentation of the Taste of Celebration check.

But first, Pepper had texted Kate asking: Coffee before the shoot?

Kate had replied: Yes, please! :)

So, that was a good sign. They agreed to meet at the French Bakery in downtown Celebration. It was within walking distance from the Celebrations, Inc., kitchen.

With Kate's positive reception, her mind shifted to other possibly more volatile topics—showing up on the set of *Catering to Dallas*.

After the debacle that she'd faced on her first day back on the set, she'd gotten the producers to guarantee in writing that her father, Harris Merriweather, would not be mentioned in any way.

Pepper had offered to stay away to ensure that focus would not be diverted from the presentation of the check, but her girlfriends and Lindsay and

Carlos, the producers of the show, had insisted that she be there.

Lindsay and Carlos had been out of town on Pepper's first day back on the show, and they had been none too thrilled when they'd heard what had happened and that Pepper had left.

When Pepper learned of the opportunity for great promotion for the Foundation and the Taste of Celebration festival, she felt as though she were contemplating walking into enemy camp. It was such a relief when she learned that Lindsay and Carlos truly cared.

Never burn bridges, she thought as she walked into the French Bakery. Nerves kicked back up when saw Kate sitting at a corner table waving at her.

Here we go. Everything is going to be fine. Shoulders back. Chin up. Everything will be fine.

Kate had the good grace to bring it up before Pepper's bottom touched the seat.

"So, you and my brother, huh? I approve. Although I'm not sure I'm a big fan of the tabloids."

Kate sipped her coffee.

"You and me both. I'm not going to lie, Kate. I can't promise you the press will stop. At least not immediately. I'm not purposely seeking attention, but to some extent it's a reality. I'm…sorry. I'm just so sorry that had to happen.

"I keep thinking things have finally settled down, and then something ugly pops up and reminds me that my life may never be the same again. But thank you for being so nice about it. I know things like that can't be good for business."

Kate shrugged. "You know what they say. There's no such thing as bad publicity. You know how to handle yourself—well, most of the time." She laughed. "Come on, we've only got a few minutes before we need to leave. Grab a cup of coffee and fill me in. Is it serious between you and my brother?"

Marjory Merriweather did not take the red eye. Her flight landed at one o'clock in the afternoon, which meant that Pepper had to take a long lunch break to pick up her mother at the airport and deposit her at home.

After much debate, she decided that it would be best to ease her mother into her new reality. What better way than having her meet her curbside at baggage claim.

While it meant that Marjory wouldn't have to trek all the way out into the parking lot, it also meant that she, who was used to having people wait on her hand and foot, would have to handle her own baggage.

Wrangling her own bags out to Pepper's car— rather than having an attendant help her to the hired car—would be enough of a culture shock. Or perhaps it was better viewed as a compromise. Pepper would've gone in to help, but she couldn't leave the car unattended.

On first glance, she felt a little guilty when she saw her mother struggling out the door with a rolling bag in each hand. But then she realized the handsome man who was holding open the door, and who looked to be about ten years her mother's junior, was also deftly handling four suitcases that matched her mother's other two. She'd managed to find help after all.

It was right there that Pepper realized she didn't have to worry about her mom. Marjory Merriweather would be fine. It was time that Pepper started looking out for herself.

Life was definitely a series of ups and downs. Thank goodness it seemed to be on an upward trend—at least for the time being, Rob mused as he let himself into the house.

Who'd'a thunk that going from the tabloids straight into reality TV would be a good thing?

The taping had gone perfectly. Kate and he had done the on-camera grip-and-grin. Pepper had watched from the wings—if that's what you called the off-camera area—before she had to leave to pick up her mother.

It had been a pleasure meeting Pepper's friends, who obviously adored her. And it had been a good exercise in relationship building. The people who ran the annual Taste of Celebration fund-raiser had agreed to donate next year's proceeds to the Macintyre Family Foundation to be earmarked for the pediatric surgical wing at Celebration Memorial Hospital.

The day couldn't have gone much better. The only thing left undone was meeting Pepper's mother. Rob was amazed that he was looking forward to it.

From the foyer, he heard the soft coo of a woman's voice and then the distinct sound of Cody's delighted giggle.

He made his way into the family room and saw Pepper reading to his son.

The boy pointed to the book Pepper was holding and growled the fiercest sound he'd ever heard come out of his son. Then he laughed delightedly.

"Do I detect a wild rumpus going on in here?" Rob stretched his arms out and did his best monster walk toward Cody, who screamed in delight and giggled when Rob tickled him.

Pepper put down the book and stood up. "Nadia had a minor family emergency, and she asked me if I would sit with Cody until you got home."

"Oh, is everything okay?"

"I think so. She said one of her granddaughters was sick and she had to go care for her."

Rob nodded. "Family first," he said, as he hung up his coat. He glanced around, taking in the Christmas lights and decorations that Nadia must've put up today before she left.

"Hey, bud, did you help Nadia decorate today?"

"Yep," Cody croaked in his five-year-old voice.

"It looks great in here. Good job."

"Yep," he repeated.

"Hey, Cody, what do you want for Christmas?" Pepper asked him.

"A wolf suit!" he cheered.

No stuttering.

In fact... He looked up and gazed at Pepper and Cody, who had returned to their reading. His son hadn't stuttered once since Rob had walked in the door.

Trying to be unobtrusive, he walked a little closer and pretended to open some mail while he listened in on what Cody and Pepper were doing.

She would read a line from the book and have him repeat it back to her, tracing his finger under the words on the page.

"Now, it's your turn," she'd say. "Say it very slowly. We want to make this book last a *long, long time.*" Very slowly, she growled out the words *long, long time* in a monster voice. Cody repeated the words she told him to say. He took his time, sometimes coming to a complete stop for several seconds to work his mouth into the proper shape, waiting until he had a strong enough hold on the word to spit it out without stuttering.

Pepper was teaching his son to…to cope with this condition that had had a firm grip on him since the accident and his mother's abandonment.

He watched in silent amazement as the woman he once worried was so frivolous and shallow helped a little boy in a way that could possibly change his life.

He didn't know she could do that.

Hell, he didn't know if *he* could do that.

But one thing he did know was that he was starting to fall in love with her.

And he had no idea what to do about that.

She accepted Rob's invitation to stay for dinner. Nadia had prepared a lasagna before she left to tend to her family.

"So, I need to ask you something," Pepper said to Rob after Cody had settled into watching his favorite cartoon on television.

"Anything," Rob said. His voice held a particularly flirty note to it. It stirred something in her belly.

"Well, gosh, this is important, but I don't know if I want to cash in my *anything* card on this," she teased. "I mean this is a pretty straightforward yes-or-no question."

He donned potholder mitts and took Nadia's lasagna out of the oven.

Rob's voice saying "Family first" when he'd heard of Nadia's need to tend to her own registered in her head. His roots really were firmly rooted in his people, which essentially boiled down to Cody and Kate. The three of them together made a family—as nontraditional as they were. In many ways, she realized, they were a firmer family unit than her own, which at one time had been considered a pillar of the Dallas/Celebration community.

How quickly things had crumbled. Her father was dead. Her mother was more distant than ever. Pepper had had a brief conversation with her as she'd dropped her off at the house, but her mother hadn't been ready to talk about her husband's death, much less discuss plans to scatter his ashes. In true form, Marjory Merriweather was emotionally unavailable when Pepper needed her most. So, Pepper tried to be patient and focused on the fact that her mother was home. She just needed time to adjust.

One step at a time. She reminded herself, family wasn't necessarily about blood as much as it was about choice. Really, the closest thing she had to family was her girlfriends.

"So, you were saying?" Rob asked.

"Sorry, I was momentarily blinded by how stunning you look in those oven mitts."

Rob mugged a pose wearing the mitts and Pepper lost another little piece of her heart.

"All right, Adonis, would it be okay if I gave Cody my brother's old wolf suit? My mom had it made for him when he was about Cody's size. Some costume designer made it. It was a pretty big deal."

Rob sobered. "It belonged to your twin brother?"

She nodded, feeling a little wistful. "My only brother." It suddenly hit her that maybe it wasn't such a good idea. "Maybe not. It's okay if you don't think it's such a good idea. It is more than twenty-five years old. So, it may not be appropriate."

Or good enough.

"I'll bet it's fabulous," he said. "My only reservation is that you might want to hang on to it."

"Well, the last time I wore Max's wolf suit was a very long time ago, and it was a very wild rumpus."

"I'll bet." He wiggled his brows at her. "I'd love to see you in a wolf suit. Although I had you pegged as more of the Red Riding Hood type."

She rolled her eyes. "Actually, I can't remember my brother ever letting me try it on." And after he died, she never took it out of its box again. But she'd kept it. She shook away the blue meanies that were threatening to settle around her. "Still, Carson and I stirred some wild rumpuses that would've made Max himself roar with envy. You'll have to ask my mom about that when you meet her."

"Yeah, I'm looking forward to that."

She paused. Really? She swallowed hard and brushed a piece of hair—that may or may not have been there—off her forehead. "You know, sometimes I look at you and Kate and wonder if that's how Carson and I would've been. You two have a great relationship. You're such a great family."

"I suppose we have our moments."

"You're not a traditional family unit, but that's what I love about you guys. You give me hope for my mother and me."

The way he smiled at her conveyed more than any words he could've spoken. It unnerved her a little and she wasn't quite sure how to react or what to say. So, when he opened a cabinet and took down three plates, she reached for them. "Here give me those."

He didn't let go, but instead pulled her into him. Leaning over the plates, he kissed her. She was very aware that it was the first time they'd kissed in his house. It felt strange and new and sort of like the first time all over again.

He set the plates on the counter and took her into his arms.

"What about Cody?" she asked.

"He's okay. I'm pretty sure he's not wearing his X-ray goggles right now."

His lips brushed hers in a feather-soft kiss and naturally, she responded, opening her mouth, letting him in. Sighing, she thought, *I could get used to these kisses*.

Who was she kidding? She already had.

He pushed her hair back and leaned in, resting his forehead on hers.

"I loved watching you in there with Cody," he said. "You're going to make a great mom someday."

She froze. Suddenly, the world tipped on its axis in the way it did when a panic attack gripped her. *Breathe. Just breathe.*

But it was still happening. She felt as if she were standing on the outside looking in on herself in this house, with this man, part of this family that somehow seemed to function despite all the obstacles that had been thrown in its path.

As much as she wanted to fit into this perfect picture, she didn't. She would make a terrible mother, just like her own mother would never be the mother of the year because she wouldn't let Pepper bridge the emotional ocean that had spanned between them. Pepper should've admitted that to herself before she fallen for a man with a kid.

The truth felt like a vine growing out of control, coiling around her, strangling her and tying her to a past she'd never be able to run away from, keeping her from a future that she would never have.

Because unlike the Macintyres, her family had started its slow disintegration the day she'd caused the accident that had killed her brother.

There had been no putting the shattered pieces back together. It was like the continental drift theory playing out in real life. A slow, steady shift, and once it had started, there was no way to stop it.

She had caused the accident that killed her

brother, and her parents—especially her mother—had never forgiven her.

She had certainly never forgiven herself.

Chapter Fourteen

Christmas was Rob's favorite time of year. But it had been years since he'd been able to enjoy it.

This holiday felt different. He wanted the tree. He wanted the turkey. He wanted the Christmas carols and the eggnog, too.

Bring it on. All of it.

Because for the first time in a long time, it truly did feel like the most wonderful time of the year.

He and Cody had gotten not one, but two Christmas trees—one for the formal living room, and one for the family room where they'd always celebrated their Christmases because it was the most comfortable room in the house.

They'd invited Kate and Pepper to come along on the great tree hunt, but they'd each begged off, promising to come over later to help decorate it and make Christmas cookies with Cody.

Now, with a blazing fire in the fireplace and the house smelling like pine and cinnamon, he and Pepper were gently unwrapping ornaments and hanging them on the tree.

Christmas carols were playing, and the scent of the cookies Kate and Cody were busy making in the kitchen filled the house with so much good cheer, Rob's Christmas cup threatened to overflow.

But it hadn't yet.

He unwrapped the laughing Santa ornament and was flooded with nostalgia. He held it up and showed it to Pepper, who had been a little quiet tonight.

"This one was my dad's favorite."

She took it from him and looked at it, turning it carefully in her hands.

"Aww, that's sweet."

He handed it back to him and watched him as he picked out just the right spot and hung it on the tree.

He sensed that there was something on her mind.

"Ornament for your thoughts?" he said.

She chuckled. "Actually, may I ask you something?"

She looked so solemn and inside herself that he wanted to make her laugh to draw her out.

"Are you cashing in your ask-anything pass?"

She stared off into the distance for a moment. "Yes, I suppose I am for this one. It's kind of a big one."

"Whoa, like a 'send out for champagne' kind of question? Are you asking me to marry you?"

She felt herself flush. Good grief, he was full of himself tonight.

"No! Of course not. Don't be absurd."

"Do you find the idea of marriage absurd or just the idea of being married to me absurd?"

She opened her mouth to answer, but she couldn't find the words. For the first time in a long time she was speechless. What was she supposed to say? *I'm not the woman who should be the mother of your child—of your children. Especially not precious Cody. I love him way too much for that.*

"Excuse me, I'm the one with the ask-anything pass."

But now he had killed the mood. Or maybe she had. Either way he was in much too good of a mood for her to bring him down with what she'd wanted to ask.

She sighed. "Never mind." She picked up her glass and started toward the kitchen.

"Wait, Pepper, I'm sorry. I don't mean to joke about marriage like that. I know it's not something to take lightly."

His hands were on her shoulders and he turned

her to face him. Then he took her face in his hands. "I'm sorry. Ask me anything. Please."

His gaze searched her face and there it was—that feeling of magnet moving steel and a pin pinging into place. Into exactly the right place in her heart. And it terrified her.

"Were you able to forgive you father for the accident?"

Now it was his turn to be rendered speechless. He regarded her for a moment without saying anything.

"Actually, yes. I have forgiven him."

"So, if he were here right now, and Cody was…"

He took her by the hand and led her to the couch. "Let's sit down."

The question caught Rob off guard. Actually, it knocked the wind out of him like a sucker punch to the gut. But this was something that Pepper needed to know and with the direction his heart was leading him, it was now or never.

He chose now.

They settled on the couch and he took a deep breath.

"There's a short answer and a long one. First, the simple answer is I forgave him because he's family. And there's that old adage that says something about how harboring resentment is like drinking poison and waiting for the other person to die."

She arched a brow at him. "That's clever. I'll have to remember that. What's the long answer?"

He raked a hand through his hair, mentally preparing himself to excavate garbage from the past that he'd buried deep in the years past. But he believed in full disclosure—keeping no secrets from those he loved.

"When I was fresh out of college, I moved to New York and got a hotshot job on Wall Street. I left my family behind and set out to make a better life for myself. Well, while I was taking care of myself, my mother died. My father blamed himself. After unsuccessfully trying to drink himself to death, he finally sobered up and decided to start taking care of Kate. She was still at home—in high school by this time. Unbeknownst to me, rather than cleaning himself up, my father had traded in one vice for another and had run up a huge gambling debt.

"He was afraid that the thugs he owed money to would hurt Kate—they actually did set the house on fire once. It was a small fire, and the fire department was able to put it out without too much damage. But it was a warning—pay up or suffer the consequences.

"My father was desperate. So he came to me. Told me they were going to kill him if he didn't pay. So I got him the money."

Pepper was listening wide-eyed and rapt. "What

did you do? Please tell me you didn't kill anyone."
She shuddered.

"No, I didn't do that, but I stole the money my
father needed."

Her mouth formed a tiny O.

"And I paid it back quickly before anyone knew it
was gone. I got lucky. And I walked away from that
world as quickly as I could because I knew what I
was capable of and I didn't like it."

"So, that's when you went and worked on the oil
rigs and worked your way up to billionaire?"

He shrugged. That wasn't the point.

"It almost seems like everything you touch turns
to gold."

Neither was that.

"No, it means that I am no better than any man
who makes a mistake. That's why I can't judge your
father or blame mine. Pepper, we all have our reasons. We all have our price and our threshold. It just
depends on the cause and how far we will go for it."

On Christmas Eve, Pepper was still thinking
about what Robert said about forgiveness. He had
been so candid with her, she wished she could be
the same.

More than anything, she wanted to ask him how
his theory of forgiveness applied to oneself.

But she couldn't. It was Christmas Eve. She'd already been Debbie Downer when they'd decorated

the tree. She wasn't going to spoil what should be one of the most magical nights of the year.

The best way to get herself in the spirit was to give presents. She'd gotten Kate an art book she'd been talking about. She was giving Rob a set of gold monogrammed French cuff links. And of course, they were both getting Maya's Chocolates. But out of everyone, she most wanted to see Cody open his present.

Rob had been in such a festive mood that he'd invited her mother, AJ, Caroline, Drew, Shane and Sydney over for a holiday toast. He'd even gotten champagne, which Pepper thought was sweet given that fact that Rob didn't drink.

It was the first time he would be meeting her mother. Pepper had to admit she was nervous. Her mother, who was used to being the grand dame, was unpredictable. She'd been thrilled by the news that Pepper and Rob were involved. Pepper had been thrilled by the fact that her mother hadn't found out through the tabloid story that had appeared after they'd returned from Orlando.

At the time, it had felt like a narrow escape. However, after she thought about it more, Pepper decided that Rob Macintyre could probably do no wrong in her mother's eyes, because, after all, he was *the* Robert Macintyre.

If Pepper dwelled on that too long, that didn't sit well with her, either. It dredged up the dread of turning out like her mother, who would, of course, be fine, but her definition of fine meant finding another rich man to take care of her.

The thought made shades of a panic attack loom large and angry. She would not be like her mother—or either one of her parents, for that matter.

She would take care of herself and not be left to depend on anyone. That resolution made her feel better.

Taking that one step further, she decided to completely immerse herself in the Christmas Eve spirit by giving Cody his present. Yes, she decided, she wouldn't wait a minute longer.

"Daddy! Aunt Katie! Pepper said I could open my pr-pr-pr…" He stopped, took a deep breath and wrapped his mouth around the word. "Present," he said resolutely. "Daddy! Aunt Katie! Come watch me open my *present*."

Pepper walked over and hugged him. She kneeled down in front of him and said, "I'm so proud of you."

She set the present on his lap and laughed as he tore into it.

Oh, to be a kid at Christmas. That's when everything seems magical.

"A wolf. Suit!" he enunciated. "I got a wolf. Suit!" He clapped his hands together in delight, and Pepper couldn't remember being happier. For a moment, she saw shades of Carson in him. Carson, who would forever live in her mind as six years old.

She took a deep breath. Cody was not Carson. He was going to grow up to live a full life. Despite his challenges. If he was anything like his father, he would one day get up and stomp right over what everyone said he could never do.

"Did you see the card?" she asked.

Cody shook his head.

"Well, it's in there. Look for it. I'll bet you can read most of it all by yourself."

He found it and tore into it with the same gusto as he'd opened the package.

"Max!" he cheered. On the cover of the card, Pepper had done her best re-creation of Maurice Sendak's beloved character. Cody studied it intently for a moment then opened it.

Cody cheered and *roar-rrrwwd,* then waved his arms like monster arms, which caused the wolf suit to fall off his lap, somehow draping itself over Pepper's shoulder.

"Help! The wolf suit is attacking me!" she cried. That sparked another round of hysterical little-boy giggles.

She put the suit back on his lap, exchanging it for the card. She opened it and pointed to what she'd written. "Look, Cody. See what I've written here?"

The boy leaned in and squinted at the print, trying in earnest to read.

Pepper traced the words with her finger. "It says, *Good for one wild rumpus.*"

"Let's have it now! Dad, I want to put my wolf suit on."

"You know what, bud? We have some company stopping by to say Merry Christmas. They're going to be here any minute. Since they've never met you, I don't want them to think my Cody is a wolf. Plus, if we have the wild rumpus now, it might scare off Santa Claus."

Cody frowned. "Hey, none of that." Rob sang a few bars of "Santa Claus Is Coming to Town," which worked as an instant attitude adjustor.

Excitement overload.

"I'll make a deal with you," Rob said to his son. "You meet our company and then you can wear your wolf suit to dinner. Deal?"

"Deal!"

Pepper folded the costume, put it back in its box and set it under the family-room Christmas tree behind the other wrapped gifts.

Fifteen minutes later, the doorbell rang. Her mother had arrived.

Pepper took a deep breath and said a silent prayer that this wasn't a bad idea. But what was the alternative? She certainly wasn't going to let her mother spend Christmas Eve alone.

Rob greeted her mother with a hug and a kiss on the cheek, which made her mother beam.

"Darling man," she said. "You are even more handsome in person than you are in your pictures."

She handed Pepper her purse. As Rob helped Marjory out of her coat she gushed to Pepper, "Sweetheart, I approve. You have no idea how I approve."

Pepper cringed.

Really, mom?

She was at a loss for how to answer, but it didn't matter because Marjory had already looped her arm through Rob's and was making her way into the living room, where Rob offered her a drink and settled her onto a chair that could've doubled as a throne.

Well, at least Marjory was in her element.

Pepper didn't know whether to kiss Rob or apologize in advance for her mother—a blanket apology for anything she might say or do that would cause offense or embarrassment.

Instead, she simply put her arms around Rob's waist and whispered, "You're wonderful."

"Why? What did I do?"

"You know," she said. "The way you're charming my mother."

"Oh, well, hey, your mother and I are already good friends."

Pepper quirked an eyebrow at him. "Really?"

"We've been talking on the phone."

Pepper laughed. "When?"

"Well, I had to invite her to the party tonight.

Since I gave all of my footmen the night off, I had to get the invitation to her somehow."

"You don't have any footmen."

"Oh, then it was a good thing I called her."

A warm glow lit her from the inside out. She adored his sense of humor, the way he didn't take himself too seriously, and now, she had to add to the list, the way he could handle her mother. Come to think about it, she adored just about everything about Rob Macintyre. A big part of her adored him because he gave her room to be herself. Room to stand on her own two feet.

The doorbell rang. The whole gang was there: AJ and Shane, Caroline and Drew and Sydney. It was so good to see them. There were kisses under the mistletoe, lots of laughter and hugging and passing around of small holiday gifts.

Rob ushered everyone into the living room, where he'd stationed an ice bucket with chilled champagne. He popped the cork and was regaling everyone with the story of Cody and his wolf suit.

"I think Pepper set the gold standard for cool Christmas presents. I think Cody would be fine if he didn't get anything else. And that's one of the many very cool things about Pepper, as I'm sure you all know."

Everyone had a flute of champagne, and it suddenly dawned on Pepper that he might have purchased it for the occasion, since he didn't drink.

She thought it was very sweet. Actually, the way he got into the holiday spirit had been her saving grace. Surrounded by all of her friends, she suddenly felt very blessed. They were her family—each and every one of them, and she didn't need more than that.

Rob was standing next to her chair. He put one hand on her shoulder and, to Pepper's surprise, he held a champagne flute in the other.

Good for him! He was allowed. His father was the alcoholic, not him. Pepper made a mental note not to say that out loud, because the part about his father probably wouldn't translate.

"I'm so glad you all could be here tonight," Rob said. "It a very special night. Not only is it Christmas Eve, but I've planned a special surprise for Pepper."

"What?" she squeaked.

"We met three weeks ago. I was telling Marjory when I was talking to her yesterday that in a way it seems like Pepper and I have known each other all our lives. Since you've come into our lives I feel like life has begun again. When it's right, it's right."

Marjory clapped her hands enthusiastically and all of a sudden, Pepper knew that her mother knew what was about to happen. Rob had talked to her. Had he asked her for...

Pepper saw everything unfold in slow motion. She had that peculiar sensation of standing outside herself and looking in on the action. That same sort of panic-attack feeling that she'd had in the kitchen last week, when Rob had told her she would make a good mother and she just felt the need to run—this time all she could see was her mother sitting there clapping and smiling. All Pepper could think was, *I can't be like her. I don't want her life.*

Rob set his champagne flute down.

He dropped down on one knee.

He took her left hand in his.

He pulled a small Tiffany box out of his pocket.

He slid the fat oval diamond onto her left ring finger.

She saw him mouth the words, more than she heard him say, "Pepper, would you do me the honor of being my wife?"

Because the majority of the sentence was drowned out by a deafening crash.

At once everyone was on their feet and Kate was yelling for Cody, but he was nowhere to be found. Not in the living room with the adults.

Again, in another slow-motion scene, Pepper ran behind Rob into the family room.

Cody's wheelchair was upended. The giant tree had fallen over on top of the little boy, who lay unconscious underneath, with his little hand clutched around the wolf suit.

Chapter Fifteen

Pepper drove Kate to the hospital. They followed behind the ambulance that carried Cody. Of course, Rob had stayed by his son's side. He insisted the others go home.

Pepper and Kate drove in silence all the way, Pepper fighting the out-of-body feeling that had settled around her when she realized that Rob was proposing, and had gone off the scales when she discovered Cody unconscious under the tree with that damn wolf suit in his hand.

Why had she given it to him?

Why had she tucked it back so far under the tree? Because she was afraid her mother would recognize it and be reminded of how one careless act from Pepper had forever torn their family apart. But her mother's demeanor hadn't changed when Rob had raved about Pepper's present to Cody. Well, of course not, she knew he was going to propose.

But she couldn't ignore the niggling voice that pointed to her that by hiding the costume under the tree, wasn't Pepper as guilty of avoidance—of not talking about the past—as she blamed her mother of being?

Her gaze dropped to her left hand, which was gripping the steering wheel at the ten o'clock position. The huge diamond glittered and winked. She had the overwhelming urge to rip it off her finger and toss it out the window.

And she might have if she'd been able to pry her hands off the steering wheel. But they were stuck at positions ten and two as she drove like a bat out of hell through the Christmas Eve fog.

She was at least cognizant enough to realize she probably shouldn't be driving, but then again, she shouldn't have given Cody the costume and she shouldn't have tucked it so far away and she shouldn't have led Rob to believe that she was ready to make the kind of commitment he was ready for— and thus continued the downward spiral.

A *ding ding* sounded from the seat next to her. She glanced over to see Kate gripping her phone, reading a text. Suddenly, Kate's hand was gripping Pepper's arm.

"He's awake. Oh, thank you, dear God, Cody is awake."

Pepper said her own silent prayer but couldn't form the words to say anything out loud.

When they finally reached the hospital, Pepper drove up to the emergency entrance to drop off Kate.

"What are you doing?" Kate asked. "Why aren't you parking?"

"I will," she murmured. "I want you to get in there as quick as possible so that Rob knows we're here."

"But I can't let you park and walk in alone. Come on, let's go. Safety in numbers."

Pepper had a flashback to the night she'd met Rob, when he adamantly refused to leave her alone at the airport. What the hell was it with the Macintyres' safety patrols? She wanted to slap herself for thinking such an ugly thought about such a kind act, but the overriding thought was, *What if Rob had never driven me home that night? If we'd never met, then Cody would be home snug in his bed waiting on Santa Claus's arrival. Not being rushed to the hospital in an ambulance on Christmas Eve.*

"I am almost positive there is a valet just down the hill," she heard herself saying. "Please, Kate, run in and let them know we're here."

Kate was not as persistent as her brother. She said, "Okay, but if there isn't a valet or if it's closed, text me and I'll come back out and walk with you."

Those Macintyres, they always stick together.

She saw herself nod yes. And drove away as soon as Kate stepped safely inside the hospital's emergency room doors.

Pepper drove right past the valet. Right out of the parking lot and onto the highway with no idea where she was going.

"What is taking Pepper so long?" Rob asked. "It's been half an hour. I can't believe you let her walk in alone."

Kate looked worried. "I texted her, but she didn't answer. Maybe we don't have a good signal in here." She held up her phone and moved it around, as if that might magically make a difference.

"She promised she would valet-park or call me to come out and meet her so we could walk in together. Let me go out into the lobby and see if maybe they just haven't directed her back here. I'll be right back, Cody."

"Okay, Aunt Katie."

"How you doing, bud?" Rob touched his son's arm. The boy was a touchstone that not every accident ended tragically. Cody was two for two.

He'd smacked his head pretty hard when he fell. From what he could tell when they moved the tree

off his son, the tree stand had failed. Cody had probably yanked on a branch when he'd leaned forward
in his chair and it had pulled the tree down on top of
him. That damn wolf suit had actually cushioned his
blow as it was somehow, miraculously, right under
his head and kept his skull from being smashed
against the travertine tiles.

He didn't mind one bit how corny he sounded
when he said it was a Christmas miracle.

Keeping it corny—because right now that was
the only thing that was keeping him from breaking
down—if he didn't know better, he'd swear his boy
had nine lives. Since he'd already used two of them,
Rob didn't want to test the theory again.

They were waiting for him to be taken in for tests
to make sure his injuries weren't more complicated
than a concussion. They would probably keep him
overnight since he'd been knocked unconscious,
but all things considered, after having a fifteen-foot
Christmas tree fall on him, he was lucky.

"Well, I guess you got your wild rumpus tonight
after all," Rob said.

"My head hurts," Cody complained. "Where's
Pepper? I want her."

Rob took out his phone and dialed her number. She picked up on the fourth ring. Just when he
thought it was going to switch over to voice mail,
he heard her say, "Hello?"

"Where are you? We're worried about you."

There was silence on the other end of the phone.

"Pepper, are you there?"

"I'm here."

"Where is *here?*"

Cody started crying, "I want Pepper. My head hurts."

"I had to leave."

Rob stood. "You left?"

Cody wailed. "I want Pepper. I want my mommy. Mommy! Mommy! I want my mommy. Pepper…"

Bad move. Way to upset Cody.

Kate stepped back into the room, and Rob motioned for her to stay with the boy so he could take the call out in the hall. The emergency room was busier than he thought it would be on Christmas Eve, and he had to walk a distance to find a place where he wouldn't be in the way.

"Okay, I'm sorry about that, Cody was crying. He's asking for you. He really needs you here right now."

"Rob, I know this is the worst possible time, but I can't do this."

"What are you talking about?" Now he was getting mad. "You're damn right it's not the time to do this. Not when my son is in the emergency room."

"It's my fault." Her voice sounded weird. Sort of distant. Like maybe she didn't understand what she was saying. Something wasn't right, and his anger morphed into concern.

"It's not your fault. Why would you say that?"

"It's like déjà vu." Her voice was definitely shaky. "It's like Carson all over again. I'm no good for him or for you."

"Oh, my God, please don't do this now. Not now. Cody is asking for you. He needs you. Please come back to the hospital."

"I can't. I can't."

"Dammit, this isn't about you, Pepper. Cody needs you. He's five years old. You don't have to stick around after tonight if you can't handle it, but at least have the common decency to help a child when he needs you."

It was the engagement ring. Too much too fast. He might feel like an idiot, but right now this wasn't about him, either.

"I caused the accident that killed my brother, Rob." Now she was sobbing. "We weren't supposed to take the horses out by ourselves. We were only six years old, but I made him. I dared him. He fell. I've got to go."

"No, Pepper, don't hang up. Cody is alive. He needs you. Carson's accident was not your fault. He fell. You did not cause that accident to happen any more than you caused the tree stand to break, which is why the tree fell on Cody. If anything, that damn wolf suit you gave him might have saved his life. His head landed on it. You actually saved him."

"I have to go," she said, and the call disconnected.

Rob muttered a string of choice words under his breath.

She was going to walk out on them just like Miranda did. With that thought a realization dawned: No matter how much he loved her or she cared for Cody—because it was obvious that she did—she was not his mother. Maybe the reason she felt as if she had to run was because he'd tried to push her into that role.

Ten minutes later, Pepper entered Rob's family room by the Christmas tree.

"You're here?" Marjory's voice sounded behind her. "Is Cody all right?"

Her mother had stayed, and Pepper didn't know what to tell her about Cody. She didn't know because she hadn't been there to find out. It had just seemed easier that way—if she didn't know, if she kept her distance, she wouldn't have to face the possibility of reliving the tragedy that had crushed her family.

All she could do was stand there and stare at her mother, mute and disengaged. That's why when her mother came over and put her arms around her and pulled her into an embrace—for the first time since she could remember—Pepper's world shifted. This time, it was a shift that seemed to help the pieces click together, rather than fall apart...for once.

All her mom did was hold her. She didn't speak or explain or try to make things right. She just held her until Pepper felt strong enough to gather up the wolf suit.

That's when Marjory broke the silence. "That was Carson's, wasn't it?"

"It was," Pepper said.

Marjory nodded.

As Pepper got into her car and drove to the hospital, she carried with her the realization that her mother had done the best she could. She was here now, wasn't she?

If Pepper didn't want to follow in her mother's footsteps, the first step she could take away from that path was to be there for Cody. That was the silent meaning that Pepper understood from her mother's uncharacteristic embrace.

It was a message that spoke much deeper than if her mother had tried to explain all the years away. They all deserved a fresh start, and Pepper resolved to not stand in the way of that happening.

Marjory was there with her in Christmas Eve. Their family was together. It was a good start.

Twenty minutes later Pepper found herself standing in the doorway of Cody's emergency room cubicle clutching his wolf suit. She'd behaved so badly, she didn't know if she was even welcome. Regardless, she had to get the costume to Cody because it might make him feel better.

It'd saved him, she thought, as she stood assessing the scene before her. Kate's back was to her as she sat holding Cody's hand. Rob looked miserable with his head in his hands. Oh, dear God, she hoped they hadn't gotten bad news about the boy—she prayed that nothing had changed since Rob had told her Cody was going to be okay.

She hugged the plush costume to her and said a silent prayer that everything would be okay. And another for her twin—or maybe it was *to* him—that she was sorry that he had to die and that she had lived.

And then the voice of an angel spoke her name.

"Pepper? I want you, Pepper."

"I'm here, baby." And she went to him and kissed his forehead.

This little angel was alive, and that was all that mattered.

Kate smiled at her. The smile of the patient Madonna-sister.

Rob looked up at her with red-rimmed eyes, and she mouthed, *I'm sorry.*

He shook his head. "It's okay."

Pepper's engagement ring glittered, and it seemed to promise, *This is your happily-ever-after.* "It's all going to be okay," she said aloud.

Because us Macintyres, we stick together.

Epilogue

Six months later

Penelope Elizabeth "Pepper" Merriweather, daughter of the late Harris and Marjory Merriweather, married Robert Lewis Macintyre on June 24 in Celebration, Texas.

The ceremony took place under the gazebo in Central Park in downtown Celebration.

The bride wore a white form-fitting gown with an elbow-length veil. She was attended by her friends and business partners—AJ Sherwood-Antonelli; Caroline Coopersmith; Sydney James who caught the bridal bouquet; and sister of the groom Kathryn

Macintyre, who took over the reins of the Macintyre Family Foundation in January, serving as the executive editor.

The groom was attended by best man, Cody Macintyre, son of the groom. The boy was able to leave his wheelchair and stand up with his father for a short time during the ceremony.

In a departure from tradition, Marjory Merriweather walked her daughter down the aisle, holding the urn that contained her late husband's ashes.

The bride and groom will honeymoon in Europe, where they will be joined by family to scatter the ashes of Harris Merriweather.

* * * * *

COMING NEXT MONTH from Harlequin
Special Edition®
AVAILABLE JUNE 19, 2012

#2197 THE LAST SINGLE MAVERICK

Montana Mavericks: Back in the Saddle

Christine Rimmer

Steadfastly single cowboy Jason Traub asks Jocelyn Bennings to accompany him to his family reunion to avoid any blind dates his family has planned for him. Little does he know that she's a runaway bride—and that he's about to lose his heart to her!

#2198 THE PRINCESS AND THE OUTLAW

Royal Babies

Leanne Banks

Princess Pippa Devereaux has never defied her family except when it comes to Nic Lafitte. But their feuding families won't be enough to keep these star-crossed lovers apart.

#2199 HIS TEXAS BABY

Men of the West

Stella Bagwell

The relationship of rival horse breeders Kitty Cartwright and Liam Donovan takes a whole new turn when an unplanned pregnancy leads to an unplanned romance.

#2200 A MARRIAGE WORTH FIGHTING FOR

McKinley Medics

Lilian Darcy

The last thing Alicia McKinley expects when she leaves her husband, MJ, is for him to put up a fight for their marriage. What surprises her even more is that she starts falling back in love with him.

#2201 THE CEO'S UNEXPECTED PROPOSAL

Reunion Brides

Karen Rose Smith

High school crushes Dawson Barrett and Mikala Conti are reunited when Dawson asks her to help his traumatized son recover from an accident. When sparks fly and a baby on the way complicates things even more, can this couple make it work?

#2202 LITTLE MATCHMAKERS

Jennifer Greene

Being a single parent is hard, but Garnet Cottrell and Tucker MacKinnon have come up with a "kid-swapping" plan to help give their boys a more well-rounded upbringing. But unbeknownst to their parents the boys have a matchmaking plan of their own.

You can find more information on upcoming Harlequin® titles, free excerpts and more at www.HarlequinInsideRomance.com.

HSECNM0612

REQUEST YOUR FREE BOOKS!
2 FREE NOVELS PLUS 2 FREE GIFTS!

◆ Harlequin®

SPECIAL EDITION
Life, Love & Family

YES! Please send me 2 FREE Harlequin® Special Edition novels and my 2 FREE gifts (gifts are worth about $10). After receiving them, if I don't wish to receive any more books, I can return the shipping statement marked "cancel." If I don't cancel, I will receive 6 brand-new novels every month and be billed just $4.49 per book in the U.S. or $5.24 per book in Canada. That's a saving of at least 14% off the cover price! It's quite a bargain! Shipping and handling is just 50¢ per book in the U.S. and 75¢ per book in Canada.* I understand that accepting the 2 free books and gifts places me under no obligation to buy anything. I can always return a shipment and cancel at any time. Even if I never buy another book, the two free books and gifts are mine to keep forever.

235/335 HDN FEGF

Name _____
(PLEASE PRINT)

Address _____ Apt. #

City _____ State/Prov. _____ Zip/Postal Code

Signature (if under 18, a parent or guardian must sign)

Mail to the **Reader Service:**
IN U.S.A.: P.O. Box 1867, Buffalo, NY 14240-1867
IN CANADA: P.O. Box 609, Fort Erie, Ontario L2A 5X3

Not valid for current subscribers to Harlequin Special Edition books.

Want to try two free books from another line?
Call 1-800-873-8635 or visit www.ReaderService.com.

* Terms and prices subject to change without notice. Prices do not include applicable taxes. Sales tax applicable in N.Y. Canadian residents will be charged applicable taxes. Offer not valid in Quebec. This offer is limited to one order per household. All orders subject to credit approval. Credit or debit balances in a customer's account(s) may be offset by any other outstanding balance owed by or to the customer. Please allow 4 to 6 weeks for delivery. Offer available while quantities last.

Your Privacy—The Reader Service is committed to protecting your privacy. Our Privacy Policy is available online at www.ReaderService.com or upon request from the Reader Service.

We make a portion of our mailing list available to reputable third parties that offer products we believe may interest you. If you prefer that we not exchange your name with third parties, or if you wish to clarify or modify your communication preferences, please visit us at www.ReaderService.com/consumerchoice or write to us at Reader Service Preference Service, P.O. Box 9062, Buffalo, NY 14269. Include your complete name and address.

*The Bowman siblings have avoided Christmas ever since
a family tragedy took the lives of their parents during the
holiday years ago. But twins Trace and Taft Bowman have
gotten past their grief, courtesy of the new women in their
lives. Is it sister Caidy's turn to find love—perhaps with
the new veterinarian in town?*

*Read on for an excerpt from
A COLD CREEK NOEL by USA TODAY
bestselling author RaeAnne Thayne, next in her
ongoing series THE COWBOYS OF COLD CREEK*

***

"For what it's worth, I think the guys around here are
crazy. Even if you did grow up with them."

He might have left things at that, safe and uncomplicated,
except his eyes suddenly shifted to her mouth and he didn't
miss the flare of heat in her gaze. He swore under his
breath, already regretting what he seemed to have no power
to resist, and then he reached for her.

As his mouth settled over hers, warm and firm and tasting
of cocoa, Caidy couldn't quite believe this was happening.

She was being kissed by the sexy new veterinarian,
just a day after thinking him rude and abrasive. For a long
moment she was shocked into immobility, then heat began
to seep through her frozen stupor. Oh. Oh, yes!

How long had it been since she had enjoyed a kiss and
wanted more? She was astounded to realize she couldn't
really remember. As his lips played over hers, she shifted her
neck slightly for a better angle. Her insides seemed to give a
collective shiver. Mmm. This was exactly what two people
ought to be doing at 3:00 a.m. on a cold December day.

He made a low sound in his throat that danced down her spine, and she felt the hard strength of his arms slide around her, pulling her closer. In this moment, nothing else seemed to matter but Ben Caldwell and the wondrous sensations fluttering through her.

Still, this was crazy. Some tiny voice of self-preservation seemed to whisper through her. What was she doing? She had no business kissing someone she barely knew and wasn't even sure she liked yet.

Though it took every last ounce of strength, she managed to slide away from all that delicious heat and move a few inches away from him, trying desperately to catch her breath.

The distance she created between them seemed to drag Ben back to his senses. He stared at her, his eyes looking as dazed as she felt. "That was wrong. I don't know what I was thinking. Your dog is a patient and…I shouldn't have…"

She might have been offended by the dismay in his voice if not for the arousal in his eyes. But his hair was a little rumpled and he had the evening shadow of a beard and all she could think was *yum*.

***

Can Caidy and Ben put their collective pasts behind them and find a brilliant future together?

Find out in A COLD CREEK NOEL, coming in December 2012 from Harlequin Special Edition. And coming in 2013, also from Harlequin Special Edition, look for Ridge's story….

When legacy commands, these Greek royals must obey!

Discover a page-turning new Harlequin Presents®
duet from *USA TODAY* bestselling author

Maisey Yates

A ROYAL WORLD APART

Desperate to escape an arranged marriage, Princess
Evangelina has tried every trick in her little black book
to dodge her security guards. But where everyone else
has failed, will her new bodyguard bend her to his
will…and steal her heart?

Available November 13, 2012.

AT HIS MAJESTY'S REQUEST

Prince Stavros Drakos rules his country like his
business—with a will of iron! And when duty demands
an heir, this resolute bachelor will turn his sole
focus to the task….

But will he finally have met his match in a world-
renowned matchmaker?

**Coming December 18, 2012,
wherever books are sold.**

ALWAYS POWERFUL, PASSIONATE AND PROVOCATIVE.

**DON'T MISS THE SEDUCTIVE CONCLUSION
TO THE MINISERIES**

WITH FAN-FAVORITE AUTHOR

BARBARA DUNLOP

Prince Raif Khouri believes that Waverly's
high-end-auction-house executive Ann Richardson
is responsible for the theft of his valuable antique Gold
Heart statue, rumored to be a good luck charm to his
family. The only way Raif can keep an eye on her—
and get the truth from her—is by kidnapping Ann and
taking her to his kingdom. But soon Raif finds himself
the prisoner as Ann tempts him like no one else.

A GOLDEN BETRAYAL

Available December 2012 from Harlequin® Desire.

HD73211